RED THREAD OF FATE

Woo Ae Yi

Word Art Publishing
9350 Wilshire Blvd
Suite 203, Beverly Hills, CA 90212
www.wordartpublishing.com
Phone: 1 (888) 614 - 1370

Published by Word Art Publishing

ISBN: Paperback   978-1-955070-00-3
        Ebook   978-1-955070-01-0

DEDICATION

To my inspiration and motivation for writing this book. To my dream and to my other dream who became my legendary nightmare. And to the dream man I didn't know I would have in my life 11 years ago

"One story featuring the red thread of fate involves a young boy. Walking home one night, a young boy sees an old man (Yue Xia Lao) standing beneath the moonlight. The man explains to the boy that he is attached to his destined wife by a red thread. Yue Xia Lao shows the boy the young girl who is destined to be his wife. Being young and having no interest in having a wife, the young boy picks up a rock and throws it at the girl, running away. Many years later, when the boy has grown into a young man, his parents arrange a wedding for him. On the night of his wedding, his wife waits for him in their bedroom, with the traditional veil covering her face. Raising it, the man is delighted to find that his wife is one of the great beauties of his village. However, she wears an adornment on her eyebrow. He asks her why she wears it and she respond that when she was a young girl, a boy threw a rock at her that struck her, leaving a scar on her eyebrow. She self-consciously wears the adornment to cover it up. The woman is, in fact, the same young girl connected to the man by the red thread shown to him by Yue Xia Lao back in his childhood, showing that they were connected by the red thread of fate." –Wikipedia, "Red Thread of Fate"

27 - And it came to pass in the time of her travail, that, behold, twins were in her womb.

28 - And it came to pass, when she travailed, that the one put out his hand: and the midwife took and bound upon his hand a scarlet thread, saying, this came out first.

29 - And it came to pass, as he drew back his hand, that, behold, his brother came out: and she said, how hast thou broken forth? this breach be upon thee: therefore, his name was called Perez.

30 - And afterward came out his brother, that had the scarlet thread upon his hand: and his name was called Zarah.

—Genesis 38:27-30

TABLE OF CONTENTS

INTRODUCTION

This book is about love between logistics. This book is about the romance and tragedies that come along with conflicting emotions of having two loves.

This book is about the romance and tragedies that come along with a relationship that was doomed from the start, a relationship between the one who makes goals and the one who makes holes. Two lovers who grew up in the sheltered, imaginative, and far off world of college moved in together, never realizing how different things would be, never realizing the difficulties of staying in love. The question: How long can they last in their own little world until they start to see the world around them?

This book is also about the romance and tragedies that come along with an age-gap relationship, a relationship in which the gap is larger than seven years. A Vietnam War veteran and a half-Korean/half-Black adoptee meet in Indiana and, ironically, they take a liking to each other. They are not just ships passing each other in the sea of life; they actually hook-up despite doubts that the relationship will work. The feelings between them are intense, making each day, each week, each month more intense than the last. But they become separated by distance. And more doubts emerge as to the longevity of the relationship. The question: How long can they last in their own little world until they start to see the world around them?

Woo Ae Yi (originally Ame Ai)
2010

CHAPTER 1

A Scam

I t was her senior year of high school. She prayed to God and made a pact with him. According to the pact, if she were to marry, then she would meet the man of her dreams in the next year. If she were to remain single, then she would not meet that man that year. Even if she did meet him, marriage would not be a possibility.

* * *

Fast-forward nine years. It has often been said that a Black man had to do twice the work of a white man in order to be recognized. If a Black man had to do that, then a Black woman had to do even more because she was doubly discriminated against. That is why when Michelle Obama came to power that most never dared criticize her (but dared criticize those who criticized her) for they understood the struggles and the accomplishments.

And so, following on that note, there was a Black woman, strong and hardworking, and there was a white man who did not work so hard and had spent such a long time working so very little that he was unemployable during an economic recession. When he did put in effort, it was in criminal activities. Despite logic, they had an eye for each other, Zarah and Perez. Here, this hardworking woman would give all that she had, including the skin off her bones if it were legal, if it would help him survive. The white man was called many names, besides the one he wanted to be called, including the prison name "Threat." There was nothing he could do for he was not only unemployable, but he was unemployable during a recession. He had an impoverished life and an impoverished future.

One day, the woman opened up her mail and received a notice that she was the luckiest woman in the world, having won millions of dollars. Even though one could say they were not hard-earned dollars, they were in a sense, for karma has a way of rewarding people. The woman dreamed and thought of what she would do with all that money, but when she fell asleep, all her dreams seemed to lead to him. She dreamt of him on his deathbed and frozen in the cold. She dreamt of him in a homeless, hippy camp surrounded by runaways and those who loved them. She dreamt of him losing his self-esteem every day and growing desperate. She dreamt of him blowing up a building because he had gotten so desperate. So, of course, her strategy had nothing to do with herself and everything to do with him.

She called her best friend, Amélie, over to discuss her idea. She explained that she could offer him a place to live at a cost, that he would have to cook and clean and do all those housekeeping chores that used to be reserved for a housewife in the days of sexism gone by. She would do this so that he had something, some sort of something that he could add to his pathetic-looking resume or to his pathetic-looking application for education. She would pay him up to $50 thousand a year for life.

Then she started thinking. She changed her mind and wanted him to be her personal trainer instead so that she could benefit from the weight loss. She would do this so that he had something, some sort of something that he could do to feel like a man.

The reason why she would not give her part of her pie was that, despite her illogical love, she had an ounce of reason and, having lived with him, she knew that he had not an ounce of understanding when it came to money and the importance of a paycheck. She had offered to buy him résumé paper and a new suit until she turned blue in the face, but he always politely declined the offer, as if it were too much of an inconvenience. She gave him gifts imbued with love, but as her money ran out, her desire to give the skin off her back did too, proportionately (though she still would have done so, if necessary).

It was her idea for them to physically separate because, at the rate they were going, she would no longer be able to afford a place for them to live or an education for him. However, they were not yet in separate homes. If she didn't have to pay the rent, she could still pay him $200 per month, which was the average of his monthly financial "emergencies."

Amélie leaned in on the phone, listening to her idea about him tending to the house or being her trainer. She tilted her head on the phone, pondering, and said, "I'm sorry, dear, but that sounds a lot like indentured servitude." And at that response, Zarah was immediately embarrassed for having thought of it and being called out for that thought by a white girl.

The woman thought for a moment, trying harder to make a quick comeback than a good answer, and replied, "No, that is more like parenting. I just want to do something. I want to help."

But the thought of what her friend said lingered long after her friend had left. She figured that perhaps that was why Reconstruction was so difficult—all these Black boyfriends were mourning for their white girlfriends who left them. Of course, that is an analogy for indentured servants and masters who were in deep relationships.

However, all this was for naught because the letter was a fake one and a scam. No money was to come out of it.

All Zarah could ever do was dream. To tell her not to dream would have been to tell her not to breathe.

CHAPTER 2

The Girlfriend

Rewind two years back. Zarah stood at the elevator and pushed the down button. No light turned on. She pressed it again. Nothing; there was no indication that it was working. She realized that in order to go down, she had to go up. Her boyfriend was in the basement waiting. She pressed the up button and got in the elevator.

* * *

Flashback…

One day it was very cold and they were waiting on a bus. He was wearing a jersey and was freezing from the cold. She wrapped her arms around him inside his shirt. They stood there like that while they waited for the bus.

* * *

Another flashback…

Zarah wanted to go swimming. She asked Perez, and he said, "Sure." The next morning, she tried to get him up to go swimming, but he was determined to sleep. She kept pulling the blankets off him to wake him up, but he used his muscles to keep the blankets on him, no matter if it did wake him up temporarily. At the time, she was amused at his determination to have things his way. He always seemed to have the power to do what he wanted to do.

* * *

When she arrived at the bottom, her eyes were wet, but he did not notice. So many flashbacks had occurred in a few moments. She had been thinking about how she missed the times when they horsed around, tickled each other, and wrestled each other, with him putting her legs in a Figure 4. One of the few things that kept her with him was that he still allowed her to rub his head in between arguments.

CHAPTER 3

Lady on a Broken Bus

Zarah and Threat yelled at each other regularly. They used to yell at each other every month, then it became every week, then there would be mood changes throughout the day from both sides. Often, she knew that something was not right and that she was not herself. She pitied herself, but mostly she felt intense pity for him. She thought that there was something wrong with Threat, but Threat often persuaded her that she was abusing him. The more she believed him, the less she believed in herself, and every red flag was lowered. She lost belief in herself and her own intuition. She believed that she was crazy and would have even killed an innocent deer, if that were considered normal, just so that she could be perceived as "normal" once again. He tended to project himself onto her and made her believe that they were, in fact, very much alike. She believed it too. He would joke that if they were both crazy, then they were crazy for each other. Sometimes he would say that they were perfect together because they were both so crazy. The only thing that was good about their anger was that they had fantastic makeup sex.

Several times she tried to leave, but all her efforts were fruitless because Threat never believed her. He would continue ranting about "unconditional love" and "abandonment," which meant a great deal to her too, being that she was an adoptee, a Black Korean adoptee. It did not take long for her to realize that to love him was to understand how God could love Satan, for she believed that he was in need of an exorcism.

The first time she was guilty of cheating on him, she only told Threat because Threat irritated her by prying into her past and asking touchy questions like, "Why don't you have Black friends?" She tried to leave. He kept her personal effects locked in his dorm room (where they used to sleep despite him having a roommate) so that she would have to get back together with him in order to get them back. When he took her back, he said that she was "worth it."

Another time she tried to leave, she still ended up driving two hours to see him. He told her that he had to cut off ties to all of her male friends, including a male friend who no one else would have been jealous of since that male friend had heart palpitations if he were turned on and had an aversion to touch. Since most of her friends were male, she refused and drove back home. He called her later that night and told her that she could keep her friends. She drove all the way back down to see him. Later, he would forget the entire situation.

* * *

Flashback…

When she first went to Notre Dame University, her roommate invited her to a party, which consisted merely of beer pong. She hardly ever hung out with her friends off the school grounds and had been indoctrinated into the belief that smoking, drinking, and drugs were BAD so she thought the party was absolutely Satanic and would have nothing to do with it. Her white dad, who was so hung up about networking, encouraged her to go for the sake of socializing, but she was not interested.

She first knew Perez as a shy football fan that attended movie showings occasionally. As has been established, she hated college parties that did not involve at least one of her sober, virginal friends. During her third year of college, Perez had to ask her out three times to a party before she said, "Yes." Perez was a persistent guy, and that's what she liked about him. She thought it was the most romantic thing he did since she had been accustomed to asking guys out instead.

Later than that she thought that perhaps she was a classic target, and he was a predator catching his prey. When she first came to his party, he had plans to lay her, she found out later. But that wasn't the worst of it; the hope that persistence for sex translated into persistence at finding a job never panned out.

The first time she saw him at the party he was under a Black light. He frightened her because his eyes and teeth looked green, and she was uncomfortable with the way he danced with her. He noticed that she was uncomfortable because she gave him a limp handshake.

They had sex on their first date. They felt so comfortable together that she stayed the next night too…and the night after that. The only time she was not with him was when she was going to graduate from college.

She did not drink or smoke until she was 21. She would not touch a drink at all until that day hit, much to the frustration of her boyfriend.

Perez's life was very different from hers. She loved the quiet and staying in on weekends. He had to have noise whenever he was not sleeping (yes, he played music loudly and obnoxiously in the car) and partied at least once a week, which just blew her mind because the most she went to parties (where there was at least one sober, virginal friend) was three times a year. It is through Perez that she experienced what is sometimes seen as the college experience, namely parties. She met many people through parties and felt very comfortable with them so that she never had any desire to drink in order to socialize, even though that was the point of the party. A month of non-stop beer pong was overkill, but being as she was able to make connections, she realized that it was equally as bad as constantly playing computer games, watching animé (Japanese animation), or watching movies.

Soon she learned that Perez smoked [weed] and that helped him know a lot of people who frequented jails. All drinking parties she had ever been to up until then had just included beer pong. And, yes, she had been to her share of "dress-to-fuck" lingerie parties. Overall, she was very thankful that she had him because he acted mostly as a mentor in this time of life, so she tried to loosen up. He made the experience of loosening up more pleasant for her so that she would not, like a reformed homosexual, condemn.

After she hit 21, college days were full of weekday house parties. College kids would keep their doors open to anyone who felt in the partying mood. Zarah felt confident about her ability to keep her grades up, so she didn't sweat it. However, she did not realize that perhaps Perez partied as an escape from keeping his grades up.

During her fourth year of college, they moved to what was called a "treehouse" on Greek Row because the dorms were named after types of trees. Oak and Willow Hall were part of the treehouses along Greek Row. A door connected the dorms. It was the "shiznit"! Willow had buyers and Oak had sellers. Willow hid a keg in the men's shower once and sorority girls found out about it. About fifty people filled each open room.

Their roommate was an angsty activist. The first thing he asked Perez was "You aren't a Republican, are you?" Perez hated to listen to his roommate's punk music, and they would often duel with their radio, particularly on their last day together. When Threat was feeling particularly mean, he would have sex with Zarah while the roommate was there.

"Drunk"
In fact, I enjoy being drunk
when I am drunk,
but I forget how much I enjoy it
when I am sober,
being able to be sober
for a long time,

that I am always wondering
which is better
for my soul.

"High on Life"
I like to live
and pretend that living is real,
and then I think
that
others
feel the same way.

"Contemplation at a Party"
I entered a party with Caucasian girls
And they seemed so beautiful in comparison with me.
But I noticed a mentally disabled kid dancing and flirting,
and they flirted back.
Why is it that so many people are prettier than me?
Yet I get the guys?
Is it fetishism? Is it racism?
And I realized that appearance
is nothing at times.
But I still look into my face in the mirror,
noting that it used to look like other faces like mine,
but not anymore,
and I asked again:
"Who are my parents?" (I hope they party)
And then I thought
this could best be expressed
through poetry.

* * *

Zarah hated Perez's lifestyle and the fact that she had to conform to it, being that they lived together, being that he wanted her to be a reflection of him. Perez hated everything she loved, like France and classic, refined entertainment. He was a francophobe, which did not really endear him to Amélie. He preferred languages that followed a consonant-vowel pattern rather than a consonant-consonant pattern. Perez loved rap and appropriating Black culture, and he despised country music and "backwards" places. She always got upset when Perez said, "Fuck country" because she was raised in Montana, but one day she realized why he said it just by asking herself "What Black country singers do I know?" and the answer was none (even though they did exist). It did not bother her as much because she got used to having few famous Black adoptee entertainers to look up to. He believed that rural places in the South had nothing to contribute to his life besides moonshine. He complained about the slow traffic and the "reverse racism" attitudes. He told her that one could tell the toothbrush was invented in West Virginia because anywhere else people would have called it "teethbrush."

Zarah was so tired of his life dominating her life. She had so many dreams that were unrealized. She slammed the door and stormed off, walking for miles until she became tired and calmed down. Not wanting to walk back, she decided to take the bus. She walked past a war zone of bottle caps and opened the door to leave. She knew that timeouts would not resolve anything and that they would just start up where they left off.

This lovely lady, who had raven hair and slightly lighter skin, boarded a typical bus with a kind Middle Eastern-looking gentleman with thick locks. On the bus, he smiled in her direction and asked, "Are you a model? You seem to have an aura about you of being a model. It is hard to describe." She blushed and contemplated, never having thought of the profession as a profession even though she did it for fun. All of a sudden, the bus stopped awkwardly, with the bus driver making noises about how they could not move because they were stuck in a ditch and that patience is appreciated. They continued talking about the bus stopping and some other unrelated things.

"So, what is your profession?" Zarah asked.

"I am a security officer. Many people say, 'security guard,' but that is incorrect."
"I don't remember seeing you on this bus."
"My car is at the shop."
"Same here. Where are you from?"
"India, on the side closest to Pakistan."
... and on and on with small talk.

The longer they waited for their unreliable transportation, which was not a surprise to the cynical passengers, the deeper was their conversation.

"How do you like it in America?" she questioned him.
"I like it. I've been here for 10 years."
"Do you live alone?"
"No. I have a wife and child. My child is very sick. We have been concerned. She is in and out of the hospital. The hospital is our second home."
"I'm sorry to hear that."
"Do you live alone?"
"Yes," she said ironically, "but I have a boyfriend who I am living with. He is very jealous, even of my male friends, of which I have a lot."
"It is a shame that someone so pretty should be tied down to a man like him."

Again, they waited for the bus, and again the conversation turned deeper, especially since they were in close proximity to one another.

"Sometimes jealousy is a bad sign," he said, "Sometimes jealousy means that you mean more to him than any other woman. It is hard to tell. Does he treat you well?"
"He neglects me, and he doesn't apologize."
"That must be difficult."
"It is. Isn't it difficult for you with all that stress?"
He leaned in, "Yes, it has been a month since I've had sex."
"It has been even longer for me."

He leaned in closer, for a whisper. "Do you like..." was all that was overheard.

"That's what I was thinking," she said with a wink.

And, well, after several hours of no progress regarding the bus, what else was there to do? She could not be criticized for her choices, being that she was a Black female and immune to criticism. Nobody on the bus really cared about them doing what it was possible for them to do as nobody really paid any attention to their conversation or what led up to this. And those who did were turned on.

When the bus finally lurched forward, they separated bodies. When he reached his destination, they parted ways. He said, "I have to get back to my wife. I hope you and your boyfriend have a good life. It was all a dream because afterwards you wake up."

When she returned to her boyfriend late in the evening, she avoided speaking with him, which was easy to do as he too was having an affair, but with a colorful box that sat on the floor all day (though she found out later that he too had had an actual affair). One time she turned it around and put a sign on it that said, in large capital letters, "DO NOT USE," but he turned it around and used it anyways.

CHAPTER 4

The Boyfriend

"Can you help me find my makeup and music? I seem to have lost it after our seventh move." (They had moved seven times in about seven months due to evictions.)

"No," he said while he was watching television.

"Why not?"

"I can't find something if I don't know where it is."

She stood there staring at him for a few moments in awe, then went back into the bedroom so that they were physically apart. Afterwards, he congratulated her on her improvement with anger management. She was really trying to improve her anger management and went to counseling to control it. He did not go because he told her that she was the problem with their relationship and that he did not need to be fixed. He also told her that she was nice to everyone but him, but then he was nice to everyone but her.

* * *

Height: 5'11"
Western sign: Scorpio
Vedic sign: Libra
Chinese sign: Metal monkey

Her complicated boyfriend, Threat, thought that she was more complicated than him and knew that she knew him fairly well. However, even though she knew everything about him, she still could not prevent or even de-escalate their frequent fights. This is what she knew about him: Everything about him returned to the desert. Everything about him returned to eczema and the fact that he has Scorpio in most of his planets. Everything about him returned to his allergies (including food allergies), his delayed puberty, his jealousy, his prowess in bed, his narcissism, and his vengeance. But, especially, everything returned to his bad luck, bad karma, and the curse of post-traumatic stress disorder from an especially tough month in jail, which was really not so bad considering the justice system's ways of sometimes keeping 14-year-olds in prison with a 27-year sentence for stealing a police car and giving someone with a 10-year sentence for robbery with a 30-year probation period. At least, that's what Amélie told her about Virginia laws in which they lived.

* * *

"Epicurean Boy"
"I know that you like me more than you love me.
I know that you need me more than you want me.
You haven't learned flexibility.
You haven't learned responsibility,
my little Epicurean boy.
You don't want to be smothered,
but you want to be mothered.
You don't need a lover, but a friend
because you tend to be lonely in the end.
But who wants to befriend a man who won't bend,
my little Epicurean boy?"

"Elastic"
"My boyfriend's into rap, but I am into Goth.
We take to the music like lights take to moths.
Choral music's best as long as it's sarcastic,
but as long as my boy thinks that rapping is fantastic,

I can be elastic.
After some time, rapping became fun.
I got used to Missy and her "budungadungdung."
Rap music's best as long as it's bombastic,
and as long as it's not monastic,
I can be elastic.
Now my boyfriend speaks of wrestling and sports.
His eyes sparkle when he talks, as if they're raspberry torts.
Testosterone is best as long as it is spastic
and as long as guys are rappers, I know it's not Barbie plastic.
So as long as it's not what I hate, I can be elastic."

"Proud"
I am proud to be your girl,
proud that you're my world,
and you need not ask why,
you just are,
like the sky.
I love you in ways I never was loved.
I was loved by a ruling stick,
hierarchy devised by a dick,
by reasons and habit
devised by tradition addicts,
and no wonder I lied
about my secrets inside.
I knew they needed grades and good standing
to justify familial pride.
But you and me, we just work,
there's not much to it.
We need not analyze/ruminate/contemplate our principles,
We lived, we prioritize, we go on and just do it.

* * *

Flashback…

Soon after Perez was born, his family moved to Bloomington, the county where Zarah's mother worked. Perez lived where her first best friend lived.

Zarah cohabited with him for a year in college, which to some is not really cohabitation. He was different in the way he thought, so nonchalant and "cool," and she was partly drawn to him because of it. He was at the same time laidback and passionate. When one hangs out with someone, different premises change, and it is so freeing to have different premises on which to build philosophies than everyone else. They were about the same weight, so when they went to sleep, they did not just sleep, they pretzelled, until 5PM on weekends.

Threat proved he missed her by his anxiousness for sex after the duration in which she was sometimes gone and not in the room at night. However, most times she would have to spend too much time in the bathroom, hugging a gallon of cranberry juice.

When she described her family to Perez he said it sounded as if they acted like she was still 13 years old. She always thought it ironic that he would choose that age because he was precisely correct. She had not told them about the traumas of high school. What she loved about Threat was actually that he loved being a white male and used that love for self-affirming definition rather than exclusion. She could not say the same for many other white men. When her father spoke about being a white male, she felt that he felt damned for being so. And as for her, she did not even know what being a Black Korean adoptee entailed. She knew so much about herself, more than most she felt, and yet she still did not know that. Therefore, her identity was never complete.

Another thing she loved about Perez was that he loved wrestling; he didn't care if entertainment had a plot. He loved Ludacris; he didn't care if songs had good lyrics (She liked Missy Elliott herself). He always got the version with explicit lyrics; he enjoyed cuss words the way they should be enjoyed. He loved Tupac; he didn't care if others saw him as ignorant or a poser, because he read Tupac's book. He was himself and that, she thought, is the best morality ever because when you attach right and wrong to your actions, without fully knowing what right and wrong boils down to, that creates hate and hypocrisy.

He also introduced her to the idea that mainstream was not necessarily a bad thing. With the combination of her thinking and his thinking, she was able to realize that the dominant culture closes possibilities as well as opens possibilities. Thinking outside the box is not really thinking outside the box; it is merely cliché. You cannot reject a new idea; you have to learn how to use it. One does not have to regurgitate or reject society's views, but one should integrate society's ideas into one's personal constellation of meaning, as one does in responding to essays.

To her, he had the "tytest" body she had ever seen. He had the curviest, most flexible back she had ever laid her eyes on. He swaggered when he walked. His head smelled like pizza or potatoes and when she told him that he said, "That explains why bulldogs seem to love me." He was about the same size as her, though slightly skinnier and with different distribution. She found this out because she tried his jersey and jeans (along with his hat and glasses) on one day and their dorm friend thought she looked like him for a split second, since he did not initially see her skin color. Even though she had had other serious boyfriends, Perez was the only boy that she slept with every day for about a year. She got so accustomed to sleeping with Perez that it made senioritis a difficult obstacle to overcome. So many times, she wanted to skip class just because she could not leave his warmth. She could not untangle herself from his legs, the smell of his hair.

He physically trapped her sometimes. He would lie on top of her; she rarely lied on top of him. His baby face, and the fact that he would sometimes rest his head on her breast made her feel like a mother, just by the way they were positioned most of the time. He would prop her up as a backrest so that he could watch television, and she did not seem to mind. She would wish that it would never end, and it was only when she had to confront the "temporality" that she lapsed back into depression.

He had a beautiful body, but his body hated him. Every day it seemed that something was sore—a shoulder, a neck, a knee. He had a skin problem that made his skin dry up.

He had eczema, a skin condition typified by dry skin. This made her realize that everyone is a medical minority. Many times eczema would leave him bedridden, and he would always wear socks because his feet were where eczema hit the hardest, but he always tried to make her take her socks off. On their first date, before they had sex, she noticed the eczema on his feet and massaged them. He said that she had the most loving hands.

It was eczema that caused him to have late puberty, a puberty that emerged during his college years. In emotional age, he was far behind his peers.

It was eczema that caused him to be the center of his family's universe. When she had a cold, she learned that he knew so much about alternative medicine because his family was always on the search for the perfect cure. The closest he could find to a cure was petroleum jelly. Zarah was close with his mother since they had the same astrological sign, and Zarah would often call her for advice. The advice she would receive was always to stroke his ego, which she could not understand, being in a world of feminism. Sometimes Threat's mother would tell Zarah what an expert she was at stroking her ex-husband's ego. His mother was glad that someone was taking care of her son.

Perez has defined himself by his family. His family lives all over the country. He had a few descendants who were true slaves, so he'd say that helped him to sympathize with Black people, but it wasn't apparent in his appearance as they were part of his tree through marriage, not through genetics, not through a direct line. She would describe him as nonchalant and in direct opposition to that aspect in his mother.

His mother was a "neat freak/control freak" flight attendant, and his father was an independent telecommunications man. His mother expected him to read her mind and continually put him in a Catch-22 situation. His mother was offended by Perez's clothes, especially if it was red because she thought it was too "wigger," though I knew red was also an Asian's favorite color, so it was not really a racial thing. Despite their differences, they had one thing in common: it was unpleasant to go home. As she listened to his mother and him battle for an hour on the phone, she realized that role models she idolized as a child could only be that way by being surrounded intimately with unpleasantness. Even though he was now 24, his mother kept tabs on him every five days whereas Zarah only spoke with her parents on holidays and school breaks. Sometimes his mother would forget that he had food allergies and would give him what he was allergic to. When Zarah was with them for the holidays, her mother treated her as part of the family, not as a guest. That meant that she got to help clean up the dishes.

His father had divorced his mother and was living with his girlfriend, an intellectual reader and traveler. When Perez and his sister graduated, Perez's mother tolerated the presence of her ex-husband's girlfriend, and her friends would tell her how brave she was. Later, that father left his girlfriend for the adventure of living in another country. She was so angry that she threw Perez's sister out on the curb who was temporarily living with them.

His younger sister deferred to her mother in her opinions and ignored Perez. She was also afraid of other people like him. She had gone through her own traumas by herself. Perhaps she did not need to be reminded of his. In certain ways, his family was much like Zarah's family. From what he had told her, his sister used to look up to him, being that he was older, but soon began to disregard everything he said. The relationship with his sister reminded Zarah of the relationship of her father and uncle. According to Zarah, her taste in music and clothing was pretty much equivalent to his sister's taste in music and clothing. His sister represented who she was and Threat represented who she had become. Knowing Threat, she knew that his way of living was the better way.

Perez was a quiet revolutionary, meaning he walked his revolution by the way he lived, not by pushing his opinion on others. Here are some quotes he underlined from Fight the Power by Chuck D.:

"The true message of the jam is don't let anybody try to hold you back from what you believe in" (p.44)

"Essential elements for the survival of the Hip-hop genre: discipline, organization, administration, and management" (p.107)

Threat saw television as necessary to daily life. He believed that television helps conversation the way that books used to help conversation in the late 19th century. His attitude toward it was the attitude most people have toward newspapers; it is a way to stay current. Perez was a sensory-heavy guy, and what a nice pairing for a poet (an imagery thinker with a metaphor thinker)! He was a visual learner as is evidenced by his major in geography and his passion for television. He related to people with his television. He kept up-to-date on contemporary allusions. He thought with literal white noise (television, music, etc.) and not figurative white noise (unsound arguments that go unchecked). He could put things in context of other things. This is no weakness. It is clarity. And clarity encourages strength.

He had a fun side too. Threat loved humor and hated being sober. Perez hated Russian literature because it was depressing and not funny. His humor was as contagious as a crowd's humor, and Zarah's daily enthusiasm for seeing him was like the daily enthusiasm of a dog. His was the surefire way of dodging depression. The first time she felt free to burp was when she was with Perez.

A lot of things can be said with comedy. Comedy is very cultural. One has to wonder if any of the exceedingly serious people of the 1600s had any sense of humor. Humor, jokes, comedy, are all very interesting because, if done the right way, it can have a very serious meaning as in satire, but because it is funny no one takes it seriously and, thus, only people who have learned that everything in this world is serious will ever understand the message. Comedians are probably the best messengers because they specialize in allusions. According to Zarah's father, the most humorous is what is the most true. If you want to find someone very honest, try to find a comedian. Perez surely watched his share of American satire. His favorite things to yell out were "What?" and "Yeah" from the Dave Chappelle Show, in which he makes fun of Lil Jon, and "Mindtaker" from Harvey Birdman. He was also good at saying "Giggitti giggitti gig" from Family Guy.

Laugh at yourself, not at others. A friendly joke can be taken personally if you're on bad relations with someone or if your sense of humor doesn't click. Why is it okay to betray our most sacred convictions for the sake of humor and conversation?

He liked to play video games on the television: one-to-one fighting games and Nintendo Gamecube, which is geared towards a youthful audience. Together, they enjoyed playing Super Smash Brothers Melee, Soul Caliber II, Guilty Gear, and Def Jam Vendetta. She played the latter by herself for up to five hours while Perez watched football. Later, she would wait alone for hours in line to get the Nintendo Wii when it first came out. That was followed by several purchases for Wii-based games.

Sunday to him meant watching football. She was interested in football once for an ex, but she lost interest again until she dated Perez. Every Monday was football and wrestling. She swore that those fans were the only people who liked Mondays. She would continually ask him what the appeal was. Finally, she realized that she should probably approach it with the learning style most appropriate for her personality: learning through metaphors. So, she finally learned to see the passion in football by comparing coaches to preachers and football stars to wrestlers (because Perez told her that one in every five wrestlers was in collegiate football). And she enjoyed watching wrestling no matter whether it was scripted. But she enjoyed it mostly in the same way she enjoyed fashion and watching breakdancing—it showcased individuality.

Wrestling was more an individual's sport, but she could appreciate teamwork in football too. Perez liked women with naturally or unnaturally tanned skin: Melina from MNM (wrestling group) and J. Lo. She wondered if he wanted a mixed baby. Perez revered muscular dark-skinned men with bald heads. He loved wrestling and his favorite wrestler was the Rock.

Threat was very straight, but not in a homophobic way, more like in a hobbyist way. What she liked about him was that he did not use his straightness to oppress her (or so it seemed), but rather he enjoyed it when she partook in his testosterone-filled activities.

His previous girlfriends were two white girls, two Black girls, and a brief encounter with an Asian girl. One of the white girls had a father who was a drug cop. She dated him for eight months. The other main girlfriend was a Black girl who wouldn't "do the nasty" with him. That Black girl was to call their shared dorm room later, and Zarah was to pick up.

No one can understand a person better than a person who thinks completely differently, but who has had basically similar experiences. This is due to the determination caused by a mix of loyalty and curiosity to figure out what makes that person tick. By being so different one is apt to make more communication mistakes, but by making mistakes one ought to learn, and the lessons learned will be more firmly ingrained out of determination.

Zarah found it strange that she met so many white people who were afraid of Black people. Perez was the only one white person she met who was not afraid of them, did not feel uncomfortable around them, or did not criticize them from a white perspective. In fact, he reveled in all things Black and even taught her to love Kwanzaa, an American holiday. She asked about his family's involvement in the 1960s, and he told her that he did not ask, and they did not tell, similarly to what she heard from a woman who worked in a Southern museum about the families in South Carolina when she went to South Carolina for spring break. He got a low grade in class for a paper about family genealogy since he did not know about much more of his family than his immediate family. Like his parents, it was not that he was secretive, but just that he did not wish to "air his dirty laundry." She found it perplexing that by the time someone was ready to open up about the past's traumas that it was already too far back to remember. Threat did not put much stock in the past, perhaps because he wanted to forget it. She put much stock in the past because she was adopted, and the past was the only way to know the truth about where you came from. Sometimes she felt his coping mechanism as insensitive to her coping mechanism, but she supposed the opposite was true as well.

They both detested censorship. He hated when cusswords were bleeped, and she hated it when censors covered up naked people, because she loved the freedom to be sexual in her visits to France, where she met Amélie. Threat was offended that cuss words offended her, and they had a long argument in which he won.

They were both introverted, but he was introverted from choice, and she was introverted from happenstance. Also, he was able to see an end as a beginning, but she was oblivious to endings entirely. He was goal-oriented and would sacrifice what he needed to in order to reach his goal. She was more interested in the journey than the destination and feared compromising her own ethical values. This generally meant that he did not find a problem with conformity for the sake of reaching his goals, but she did. Threat would say that she didn't have initiative.

Threat was a Baptist. He went to a Southern Baptist Christian school growing up and was more knowledgeable than most about the Bible. Even Satan knows the Bible.

His wardrobe was a "wigger's" wardrobe. He had a choice of beanie or ballcap, t-shirt or long-sleeved shirt, sweatpants or jeans, and tennis shoes or tan work boots. He would always give her Tommy Hilfiger clothing for gifts, as if clothing could neutralize skin tone.

He liked rap as well as Japanese music. His favorite musician was Ludacris, and his favorite animé was Naruto. Threat truly enjoyed explicit modern rap (which had been getting an...ahem...bad rap). As long as it was not 50 Cent. He also liked the Kings of Crunk album by Lil Jon and the Eastside Boys. He was fearless, and his fearlessness showed in his interests. He has opened many white people up to rap. The thing she liked about his acquaintances was that most of the males preferred hard music to soft music. Perez listened to rap, his friend listened to Tool and Perfect Circle, and his other friend listened to heavy metal. His favorite teacher was a former Black Panther, and the only teacher who rapped. His least favorite character was Carrot Top. However, beyond the Black culture stuff, she thought he had an inner nerd. He has watched animé since eighth grade.

Outwardly, he hated repeating himself. Inwardly, he just hated himself.

Perez could easily sleep 24 hours if given the chance. As he was carefree and a sports fan, he tended not to analyze much, so it was a good balance. His priority was sleeping and though he was what one would consider lazy, she did not see it as a sin. Laziness is only a hindrance to a relationship if the other side is not willing to cater. His laziness was not a laziness of not caring (apathy), but a laziness of not wanting. In his mind it was fine to work hard but only if you care about the cause and the leader; if not, then hard work is worse than laziness. Surprisingly, he did not like lazy girls (though she thought he was referring to laziness in bed).

He was not the curious type, the talkative type maybe, but as mentioned before, they did not talk too much about the past. Sports enthusiasts tend not to be as curious as art enthusiasts she noticed. At first, she was frustrated because she wanted a listening ear, but then she realized that life was far more pleasant than if one dwelt on it. Sometimes they did not quite understand each other. He did not understand why she would watch movies and read books that no one else she knew has read.

Zarah's mother accused her of deferring to him, but she saw that statement as hypocritical since her mother changed her political party when she married her father, and she still defers to him in all things political, even if it were to lead her into a cult.

As for his friends, his drug dealer friend was a storyteller and a rugby player who (it goes without saying) had a high tolerance for pain. He called Perez "Token" since he was often the only white man in a sea of Black. His favorite song was "Fiddle and the Drum" by A Perfect Circle. His other friend was also a rugby player, but he was also a music major who hits on Zarah when he was drunk. That "friend" was jealous that "Token" was so close to the drug dealer and turned others against him.

One day Zarah asked her friend, a seasoned tarot card reader, to give them a tarot reading. They found out that Threat was the Sun, and she was the Empress. For his reading, there were many cards that included the number two or spears. In Zarah's reading there were many cards that included the number seven and shields. In Threat's past lives he was an all-around "badass" before he became a mediocre military-leader-turned-advisor and then became a female spiritual leader. From the previous tarot reading her friend gave her, she was a geisha for one man, then bedridden, then a traveler because she was sick of being bedridden. In the second tarot reading, the one with Perez, she was a loner from happenstance who was killed just because the people around her did not know her, then she was a scholarly male in a monastery, then she was a traveler (she wondered if this was the same life as in the tarot reading before). She got the impression that from all of her lives she never felt any closure or answers to any questions and always felt stagnant and bored. Even in this life she had a boring, stable childhood. Since the wheel of fortune came up in the cards it also gave her the impression that she got where she was out of luck more than anything else.

In more detail, the cards said that Perez's personality was introverted, practical, job-oriented (ha!), and optimistic. Also, he learned best with field trips. His main problems were that he put off decision making in lieu of partying and that he tended to internalize feelings and decisions and needed to share his emotions and the decision-making process more. Her personality was relationship-oriented and such that she seemed impulsive on the outside, but her choices were very well thought out before she made the split decisions. Her problem was that she felt a time limit on being able to go on a path in which her life would not end up as stagnant as she felt that it was.

His past included a household where the house could explode any minute, and he had no hand in it, so he often tried to escape. Her past included early trauma and prison, which she suspected meant the time she was in a crib in the first few months of her life before adoption. His career was where he would shine (ha!). Her career was where she had to be careful not to keep all information to herself, which she keeps forgetting. His love life included her, but she was more a long-time friend and just another thing to complicate the decisions he had to make (this was a curious thing to her at the time). Her love life was more about her understanding herself through relationships than about anyone in particular.

Zarah, knowing some about palm reading, would also note in the back of her head that he was in the beginning of his reincarnation cycle, and she was near the end. He would not meet with much success, but she would. Strange, she thought, why do we not have success together?

Their love song was "Chasing Cars" by Snow Patrol.

Overall, when it came to Threat, her greatest fear was marriage. She believed all men would wind up having a temper since her mother had no idea what she was getting into when she married her father. She believed too that all men who have a temper would inevitably show their temper to their child just because that is what bullies do; they pick on those who cannot defend themselves. And as much as she cared for Threat, she knew that she would see that repeat, that when she was emotional that the stress in the house would cause someone she did not know to come forth and stay.

"Reminder"
"Friendship comes and goes. Depression is forever"
is a true statement.
In an unexpected flash of sirened agitation,
My life flickered
And made me wonder why I felt pressured
Into giving time to
"Feel good" bodily acquaintances.
How easily does the carefree eye
Turn,
How quickly does
Sweetness succumb
To transiency like body of yours,
And sometimes like vows.
A life this easy
Cannot exist.
A life this easy
Cannot be remembered for long
By anyone else but a sponge—like me,
Passively staring at cyclical repeating,
Non-participatingly and intentionally obliviously,
Giving nothing but time (which Dad says is the best gift to
Give) and
Taking everything, not in cruelty, but in
Admiration, an admiration tacked to
Dependency that
Gives
Nothing to myself.

CHAPTER 5

Zarah's Parents

When Zarah met Perez she had nothing but good things to say about him. When her father found out that he worked at a gas station, he had nothing but bad things to say about him and refused to meet him. She turned on her father. Her father turned on her. Her mother was caught in the middle and was often lumped with her father in Zarah's mind.

Her mother got a chance to meet Perez during a women's church retreat. Zarah received a call from him. He did not express that he had depression, but he was certainly depressed. She told him that he could visit her. He drove up to see her. Her mother had left her umbrella outside. He drove to retrieve it and, in attempting to retrieve it, got his car stuck in a ditch. He stayed with Zarah in her mother's car while they waited for AAA. He would later cite that as the most romantic thing he had ever done for her even though he did it for her mother, whereas Zarah would cite paying his rent the most romantic thing she had ever done for him. It was not until even later that Zarah would acknowledge that, for him, it truly was romantic and selfless. The next day at the retreat she was to receive a necklace that was to be a sign unto her. "True love waits" was emblazoned across the front of a cross pendant. It wasn't until later that she thought to emblazon it across her flesh.

They knew that something was seriously wrong when her father discovered that Threat had smeared his feces on the inside of the bathroom door. Zarah did not believe her own father when he put his hand on the Bible and swore that he did not make it up. That was what made her sever ties with her adoptive parents, not the reason why most adoptees sever ties.

Threat knew about her adoption and told her that her adoptive parents were the bad guys and that she needed to find her biological family, which he knew deep down would never happen.

Zarah forced that memory out of her mind and refused to speak about it.

CHAPTER 6

Saturn

When Threat was neither fighting with her nor watching television, he would help her with extreme exercises, like 1,200 sit-ups daily, because she had too much weight. They did this every day because it was the only way to get fast results. Zarah would suggest something fun, like dancing, but he did not believe that exercise was supposed to be fun. When she told him that he wants her to be skinny, he denied it and reminded her that she was not as skinny when they started dating. The next time her mother saw her she was to tell her that she looked like a skeleton.

He controlled her body in other ways as well. He told her to shave off her pubes and wear only thongs. She hated to do both and when she did the former, she was not happy with herself. But at least she pleased him.

She had always been an obedient girl, but sometimes she felt not good enough. She wished that she were more domestic, more traditional. She wished that she could "serve and obey" better. If she could not behave, then he would never marry her.

* * *

Their neighbor was an old astronomer (or was it an astrologer?). He mentioned that something big was going to happen, something about

Saturn returning. He was telling an older woman (perhaps his wife?) about this phenomenon and about the dramatic changes it can bring about, but only in one's late 20s or early 30s.

One day after her romp in the bus, Threat overheard his girlfriend singing a song that she made up after a serious argument about nothing that important. In fact, every serious argument they ever had was about nothing important, and somehow, that made the unimportant a matter of living together or living apart, a matter of him killing her or her killing him or both of them killing themselves in an alcoholic-induced Shakespearean way.
He overheard his girlfriend singing:

"I know how to love.
I know how to love myself.
I know how to care
without hurting anywhere.
I know how to love.
I know how to stand my ground.
I know how to stay,
and I know when to walk away.
I know when I need
something that's not given to me.
I know how to smile
after many a trial.
I know how to love.
I know how to love.
I know how to love."

His eczema flared up that day, and he groaned in agony over how his wife was still strong even though she was hurting and struggling in this relationship. He was jealous that she understood something that he struggled to understand. He stood outside looking thoughtful while all he thought about was what had happened to them. He realized that God's greatest blessing and curse upon mankind was that others would remember us by how we lived.

CHAPTER 7

The Second Arc

Much happened in the short time between Zarah's parents' birthdays, or, more specifically, a few days after her mother's Taurus birthday (May 15th) to seven days after her father's Scorpio birthday (December 28th). The second part of this story is about a strong, sexy man who supported her own dreams and goals and who gave her more dreams and goals. This is about a man who always accepted her the way she was despite her flaws, who understood her nature and how to respond in a way to complement her, who is honest and compassionate. This is about a man who selflessly gave her what she needed. However, she must begin at the beginning, before such concentrated excitement began.

*　*　*

It is the first of the year: New Year's Day. It was also her first day on the job at a car manufacturing shop. A blue-jeaned stranger in the hallway greets her with "Bonjour" because she was wearing a shirt adorned with the Eiffel Tower. Later, he walked to her desk, sat down, and greeted her with another French greeting, "Salut." This interesting man intrigued her. She wanted to know more. She did not have the time to ask him questions by the time he walked out the door.

Her coworker walked her around the office and downstairs in production. One of the first people he introduced her to was the interesting gentleman who greeted her. His name is Yue Lao, and he was one of a kind. She was stunned into silence by his locks of white and his almond eyes, having now had the chance to appreciate them. He wore his hair swept back, parted in the middle, like a stud from the '50s. He stood tall above her with his skin slightly lighter than her own from a tan. She smiled brightly as his eyes reached into her soul (though at that time he was really undressing her with his eyes). They smiled back at each other so long that her coworker looked back at her, and then slightly glanced at him. She and her coworker moved along to the next important person to meet. She was not to know it, or perhaps she knew it and did not utter it or think it aloud, but that chance encounter was her love at third sight. She says jokingly, she is not so naive to fall in love at first sight, like a lovestruck puppy.

One time Zarah and Yue talked a little about each other. At this encounter, she learned that he was a Vietnam vet for China, even though Beijing denied U.S. allegations of Chinese involvement.

"What was Vietnam like?" she asked, never having been before.
"Being there was an adventure. I was only 18 years old, and the world was all new to me."
"There aren't many Chinese people in Petersburg."
"But there are a lot of Asians in this company in Evansville. We have Cambodian, Thai, Koreans…."
"I'm actually half-Korean."
"Then you would be included in that."

She did not know when it started, but he boldly flirted with her as no man she has ever met. He was king of the one-liners and knew his way around pick-up lines. In addition, he winked at her a lot. He often had a twinkle in his eye. No one really winks nowadays except for that one time when she winked at the man on the bus. She asked about Yue around the office, and people told her that is just the way he is. Every day she would go to work, happy for one to be away from home and happy to hear one more interesting and piquing flirtation said in a few words or less, something so quick that even a coworker would miss it.

She cannot remember all the things he said to her. Every day it was something different, something creative. At other times, he would just say something nice and pat her knee when no one was looking.

* * *

One time during a cold, she complained that she felt miserable. "You look fine to me," he said. She perked right up.

Another time she said, "I don't like how these safety goggles make my nose look."
"You have a cute nose," he said.
He asked, "You have a master's degree, so what are you doing here?"
"I just graduated and was looking for an adventure. I have always lived in Montana. Is that ruby?" Zarah asked, pointing to a ring on his left pinky finger.
"Yes," he looked down and saw that she had a similar ring too, "I see you have one too."
"It's a birthstone given to me by my family. I'm a Cancer. What is your sign?" she asked out of curiosity.
"I'm a Leo."

Later, when she was making measurements to see how much paint was needed to cover the walls, he noted her precision. He would have made round guesses, but she had to get the measurements to the most precise quarter-inch.

"You are gorgeous for someone who is about 35," he said with a question inflection to indicate that she correct him.
"I'm 25, almost 26."
Surprised, he said that she was still gorgeous. Most people are flattered when people guess too low, but she thought maybe he guessed high so she was in an acceptable dating range for him.

* * *

She was with someone else, but she did not want Yue to know. However, after being mad at her boyfriend for meeting her at work one day, she went down to the parts room only to find that it was dark since most people's shifts were over. Yue was there by himself, closing up shop, so she confided her frustration to him, she just felt that she could trust him with her emotions even though she initially did not want him to know that she was dating someone else. She was just so... frustrated with that someone else.

"I do not have much money," she complained, knowing that when she does it disappears.
"You can always ask me for money if you need help," he told her, "Where do you live?"
"By the university. Thank you," she said appreciatively, not knowing that he did not have much money to share.

He talked to her about the streets, sounding very knowledgeable. She admitted that she had no sense of direction. In other senses of the word too, she thought bitterly.

Sometimes, when she walked downstairs, he would come up behind her and jostle her shoulder then wink at her.

* * *

One time, she tried to coordinate a get-together after work. She wrote up a memo and included some names of people she got along with at work. He sighed as she told him, explaining to her that they no longer do such things. People do not get along with each other. People want to go home after work. Things are very informal. Not a restaurant, but a bar. In amusement at her lack of knowledge, he said, "You are gorgeous," not just meaning her looks.

She invited about ten people to that event. Only Yue and his office friend plus wife came. She did not say much. There was not much to say. Afterwards, when the other two left, he winked at her.

* * *

One time, she saw him around the filing cabinets, and they talked about anonymity. He told her how it is priceless. He told her she should remove the bumper stickers from her car. It looks exceedingly tacky. He told her that his daughter was once issued two social security numbers and that he had two passports. His ex-wife, though, felt that she had to report that a mistake had been made and so one of the social security numbers was removed. He scoffed at his ex-wife. Marriage was not for him.

"I do not trust the government," he started.
"I saw a homeless man today who was wearing a nice work outfit, as if he had been newly evicted. Poor guy. I'm glad it's not me."
"This is the USA! That can't happen here!" he said ironically, with a ball cap on his head with the letters "USA" emblazoned across the front.
"Do I hear sarcasm?"
"A big fat YUP," he said, "I'm going to retire and move out of the country. I am going to move to Panama. Let me recommend something for you to watch."

* * *

He was always recommending something for her to watch. As Yue was recommending something for Zarah to watch, Threat was recommending something for Zarah to hear. After their fights, he would send her sad and angry Kanye West songs, always Kanye West. He used his senses a lot, especially seeing and hearing, all of them except for his sixth sense and intuition.

* * *

As she was helping a coworker take inventory of the parts room, Yue's lair, he teased her, telling her to beware of the "Latin lover" who was helping her, his friend. Earlier, he teased her about a Cambodian coworker, telling her that that co-worker was in love with her. Perhaps, in his jokes, he was projecting himself onto them. When her counting partner took a break from inventory, Yue took over. He called out numbers quickly, not letting her get all the details that her more precise counting partner had given her. He was like that from time to time, a little brusque.

* * *

Later, she asked him curiously, "You said that you have an ex-wife... Do you mind if I ask why you broke up?"
"Children," he told her. He was no longer needed in the house. He married around her age, separated in his thirties, and divorced in his forties.

Another time she asked him again, "Why did you break up with your ex-wife?"
"Vietnam," he told her. Times were hard, times were stressful, so much happened in a brief period of time.

* * *

Things were not always just flirtation. They felt comfortable telling each other anything. He would tell her when he was very upset at work with spatterings of the f-word. Strangely, that was endearing to her as he was not uptight or rigid like some other people are about sensitive words. He did not like authority and told her how he would get annoyed when told what to do or how to do his job.

* * *

She had an accident one day due to the icy weather because her boyfriend asked her to get alcohol to celebrate their fourth anniversary. "You are now part of the Indiana club," the office secretary told her.

She told Yue, and he instantly made things move for her. He hooked her up with the right car repairmen from the production area. A job that would have cost so much money did not cost her a penny. She was so thankful to him for that. He is a good, good man. That she will always believe. Another time the V-belt on her car broke, and she got it repaired again for hardly any cost at all.

*   *   *

"I am going to be moving the beginning of March," she said another time, remembering his familiarity with the town and surrounding towns, "I will have to drive a different route to get to work. Can you help me with directions?"

"Sure," he said as he brought up Yahoo! Maps. He spent quite a bit of time explaining to her and printing maps out for her to use. Unfortunately, when she drove according to what he wrote on paper, he had forgotten to add a few compass directions. Therefore, she had to do some guesswork.

"Didn't I hear that you had just moved again not that long ago?" he asked inquisitively. She told him how many times she had had to move while carrying deadweight over her back.

"You need to stop living like a college kid," he told her, "Here. I know someone who works at a leasing office. Tell her you know me." She called that number, and it was no longer a working number, but she never told Yue that.

"Can I borrow some boxes?" she asked.

"Yes."

"And can you help take them to my car?"

"Yes."

He paused. "Does your boyfriend treat you okay?"

He asked as he helped her move moving boxes into her car.

"Yes," she lied.

She did not bump into him for many days, and she became worried that it was because she lied. She did not really think too much of it though; she had so many problems at home.

She guessed that he wanted to know more about her too. She was to find out later that he would go into her room at times when she was stuck at home just to look at her framed diplomas. Harmlessly curious, like her.

CHAPTER 8

Mutilation

Her current boyfriend cut her, in every way, when she tried to break up with him for the fifth time, a time after she got on the floor, grabbed his ankles, and refused to let go until he would break up with her. All her attempts to escape him failed. She thought that he could not stand the idea that no one would bring him money on which to live. He kicked her in the stomach and took a kitchen knife to her eyebrow and her ankle. He stopped after she said, meekly, "Can you stop hurting me?" She still bears the scars from the cuts to this day on the outside of her right ankle and her eyebrow.

Afterwards, he was on the phone with his mother. She did not know what had happened but knew that a fight had occurred because Zarah wanted to leave. His mother was actually taking Zarah's side, but the entire time Threat was asking his mother to take his side and to see things from his point-of-view.

When her hosts came in, they said they should take their fights outside. Yes, this entire time their house was never theirs; they would never be able to return to home since they had none. Things had grown tense in the house since one of the hosts worked from home and was able to report to Zarah that unemployed Threat never tried to find a job and would steal her credit card to buy food. He would also get up to take long baths so that his hosts did not have time to get their shower before work.

She told them she cut herself. After all, he only cut her because he was tired of seeing her cutting herself, which she only did in front of him because he was the only one whose attention she craved. She literally could not stand from the wounds to her Achilles' heels. She revealed the blood. Oh, the blood! Gasps! They became concerned about her wellbeing, not understanding why, if her boyfriend knew, he would not tell someone. She thinks she could have died had they not taken her to the emergency room. Her parents swear it was possible. The pain she endured in the emergency room was excruciating, even though they were trying to fix her wounds. It took her two weeks until she could return to work and two more until she could walk like a normal person.

She was put into a hospital gown in sterile room with a woman who slept, snored, and awakened with a brain problem. She was uncomfortable.

Her hosts visited her, comforted her, and she told them about how much the relationship she had with her boyfriend was just not working. Her hosts brought her home, to their home, with pain medication and some anti-depressants. When her hosts brought the TV from downstairs up so that she could watch it, her boyfriend complained and muttered. He lived off that TV. She thought that he loved that TV more than her, and it was not even his. The time he spent watching it was time their hosts spent paying for it. He was a bad guest, to say the least.

However, she was a foolish girl. After some talking, after emotional outbursts, the couple decided that they should separate again. She would go to Maryland and stay with her best friend, and he would stay in Indiana, while they tried to sort themselves out. They would return to each other after a year's time. They believed their love was strong enough to survive. However, he said he could not stop hearing the song "Black Hole Sun" by Soundgarden.

Somehow, the perfect idea of separation never happened. At the idea of separation, even though he physically hurt her, she clung to him. What was she afraid of? The man who cut her apologized immediately (What was I doing?! he thought) and tried to endear himself to her as he helped her with everyday activities, since she was immobile and incapacitated. He apologized, and she immediately forgave him, to the despair of her hosts. She didn't tell her hosts the truth until over a decade later.

They ended up moving out of their host's home to an apartment. He believed they were back together. She believed she could not do anything drastic until she could walk without help lest she not ever be able to walk again. He was a much better boyfriend it seemed, temporarily, since she was not able to, or had lost all desire and energy to, clean up and fix meals. He took care of the food and the house, for a short time.

It took a dramatic change to learn an honest truth. To her, love was not about fighting against those who are against your lover, but about fighting against yourself when you are against your lover. And sometimes love was about fighting against your own forgetfulness when you forgive your lover. Sometimes love is about leaving.

She thought to herself, the funny thing is that we both used to be human at some point. It was very hard to remember during the thick of things, but it was clear as crystal in hindsight. When we were born, we were both pure of heart and innocent. He had infinite potential, a potential that I believed in past too long. I always prayed for the resurrection of his potential. He was cursed with incapability, an incapability to love me the way I wanted to be loved, an incapability of rising above circumstances. The more I prayed for him the more he rotted from too much exposure to his own thoughts, from too much exposure to my select thoughts. He listened to one-fourth of what I said and none of what I meant. Praying harder only made the disintegration happen faster. There was nothing I could do. I had prayed too much. But it was the only thing I could do.

CHAPTER 9

The Flirtation

Returning to work with casts on her legs, Yue replied differently to all the others who asked her questions. He jokes, "I bet that's from having too much sex" as he rocks his body like Elvis.

She smiled coyly and said, "You are so bad."
He agreed with a mischievous smile.

However, she happened to be dating someone else who she had been with for years, and her guilty conscience caught up to her. Clunking down what sounded like diamond-plated stairs, she sought him out in his parts lair. "No more flirting," she told him.

He said, "Don't make a mountain out of a molehill." In hindsight, she wished she took that advice.

She went upstairs and told her coworker that she put down her foot. She was, after all, dating someone else. She told him what Yue said. Her coworker said that it did not sound unlike Yue, but that Yue definitely must like her. "Beware though," he told her, "he is a user."

When she returned home, she told her boyfriend proudly that she turned down another man's advances, while he did not know the real feelings in her heart.

CHAPTER 10

The Beginning

The next day, after everyone has left, she was in her office to make up time she lost due to a doctor's appointment. Yue was leaving late and walked past her door. "Wait," she called out to him.

"What? I need to pack for a business trip," he said.
"Just a second. I want to talk to you. Sit down."
"No thanks. I need to leave soon."

After much verbal hesitation of pointless fillers, she finally came out with what was on her mind.

"I am conflicted because I like you. If you had me," she asked, "what would you want to do to me?"
"That is up to the woman," he said.
"Good answer."

He punctuated the conversation with tangential issues, avoiding the situation at hand. He asked her questions of unrelated matter, such as "What really happened to your leg and your eyebrow?"

"Nothing," she said evasively. "Sit down," she insists.
"No, I'm fine standing."
"My sex drive is higher thanks to you," she told him secretively.

"That's the point, I suppose," he said without showing too much emotion.

"Sit down," she said a third time, hoping to be able to catch a kiss or some emotion. He shook his head.

"We'll work things out," he said as he came near her. She tried to kiss him, but he dodged her lips, then he held her hand instead while they played the opposite of footsies with their hands.

"This is uncomfortable," she said, referring to how hard it was for her to come out with things.

"Yeah."

CHAPTER 11

The Secrecy

She dialed 411 Information so that she could find Yue's number. She greeted him on the phone. He replied in kind.

"Where are you?" he asked. She explained to him that she was in her apartment complex, outside the room she shared with someone she would rather not mention.

"I want to have sex," she blurted out unashamedly.

"Do you have protection?" He asked.

"No, I cannot afford it every month," she said, misunderstanding the question, "but I will figure out something." Birth control was expensive, and she could not afford it while trying to raise a man trying to be a boy. She somehow felt that if she were to get pregnant it would help him grow up.

"Are you curious as to how I got your number?"

"No, you can find that out easily."

"Every minute seems so long," she complained. He voiced his sincere agreement. Chemistry zapped through the airwaves.

Throughout this time that they lusted over each other, she could not help but touch herself many, many times. Her pulse would rise so much that sometimes her toes would go numb. She squirted inadvertently in the bathtub. Her boyfriend liked it, thinking that she was thinking about him. Her boyfriend always thought very highly of himself and hated whoever would put him down.

CHAPTER 12

Lust

"Querpo"
Quiero estudiar
tu cara-tu ojo, tu nariz, tu boca, tu orejas
tu mano-tu dedos, tu muñeca
tu muslos, tu ingle,
tu nalgas, tu testiculos, tu pene

Quiero lavarse
tu corazón

After he returned to work, they were all over each other in-between the shelves in the parts room, with each minute making their temperatures rise, their excitement escalate. They grabbed at each other lustily, wishing that they were in a bed, wishing that they could throw each other's clothing on the floor. They ravished each other and uttered stifled, but uncontrollable moans. Every time they dared to tear at each other's clothing without completely taking it off, she would tell him that she had never felt so horny in all her life and asked him too: "Have you ever felt so horny?" The first time they groped, unsure of what was too far. He suckled at her breast. She took in his wonderful fragrance, a smell she will never forget, and made love to his neck with her kisses. Their eyes kept moving from each other to the rest of the world, hoping for their privacy. The next time they had a lunch break, she tried to suck him. The next time she wanted him in from the back. However, it is a dangerous game that they played. They could be caught.

At the lunch break, she went downstairs. He was not there. She waited for him in-between the shelves. She saw him. She pulled his shirt toward her, dragging him along with it. He grabbed at her jacket and pulled her in too, as he kissed her. He took a flattened cardboard box and held it up near her head, hiding their faces from the world.

It had been almost fifteen minutes one time (he was always so good at telling time in his head, because he didn't wear a watch, he would tell her later), and he indicated that she should get back to work. She left, bumping into someone as she walked up the staircase. Yue had perfect intuition.

Throughout that week, she arranged her schedule stealthily so she could see him, noting where to place doctor's appointments, so that she could tell her current boyfriend lies. She told Yue that things should be fine. It is, after all, football season, either the draft or the play-offs; it did not matter.

"Do you like sports?" she asked.
"Not at all," He told her.
Ecstatic she said, "Thank God you don't like sports. Me neither."
She thought about how her own boyfriend needed a football fan to complete him.

One time as she went downstairs, he hid her behind large industrial equipment, out in the open, not like the shelves, and he grinded up against her as they kissed with no one around.

As they made out, he whispered, "Tonight, I will be all over your body." As they made love, he hurriedly wrote down how to get to his place from work. His handwriting was his, all unique and lovable. His hurried penmanship created many boldly angled letters. She saved his handwriting. The night they planned to make love did not work out.

Her boyfriend wanted to go to something that lasted too long into the night. Nevertheless, as soon as she could the next day or some days after, discreetly, she met Yue at his home.

"Feel my heart," he said, "It's racing." They were nervous as hell. However, he licked her just right. "I have dreamt about this," he would say.
"Yue, oh, Yue!" she moaned.

In addition, they made love in a way so that she knew he was worth keeping, despite her intention for this to be a one-night stand. She was still with someone else, after all. She feels that sex says a lot about a person. Her boyfriend always preferred to be a taker because that is just the way he is, like other young boys. But a man, oh a man who likes to give and receive... Sign her up!

"I do not want to go to sleep; I want to bask in this moment," she'd say.
"Go to sleep. We have to go to work in the morning."

The next morning, she looked around at his media collection with fascination and interest. It showed her a little bit of the man she had made love to. She took in everything: the open door that let in the morning air, the collection of Vince Flynn novels, the location of his alcohol, the pictures on his wall of his family, of himself.

He showed her what he looked like when he was young. He did not look at all like what he looks like now. He had dark, permed hair. She told him, "I think you are more attractive now; I would never wish you to be younger." As she looked at him when he was her age, she knew that she would not have sought him out. He showed her his former passports and the progression of age. As he showed her his progression of age through his passport photos, she concluded that he was like a fine wine, getting only better with age. Moreover, she was just another thing to help him build his character, to help him be sexier, to add boldness to the flavor of his body.

As she filled in for the secretary who was on vacation, he would come by her desk briefly, put his elbows on the desk, and tell her that she should not shave; "It is scorched earth down there," he said. And you know, the strangest thing came to her like a light. She felt it was a sign that she could be herself. She could not tell anyone how hard it was for her to shave, at her boyfriend's insistence. She felt she had compromised too much of herself in that one act. She had compromised her body and handed it over to someone she did not even love, someone who did not love her, someone who used sex as an answer to all relationship problems.

"I can't," she whispered, "My boyfriend would know."
"He likes it shaved?"
"Yes."

She would keep track of when Yue took late lunches. When he came back in from the outside, he would smile at her, like a schoolboy, and her like a Cheshire cat.

"Next time we have sex," he whispered to her, "I want to put the spermicide on you."

*　*　*

One time he came by and she got between him and the fax machine. She did not know what to say but tried to look sexy anyways. He laughed. God, she loved that laugh.

*　*　*

She was learning things about him too while she lusted for him. She saw him with a black t-shirt and noticed eczema on his elbows. He normally wore a long-sleeved blue jean jacket that covered his elbows. She was familiar with eczema. Her boyfriend shared the same problem.

*　*　*

"When is your birthday?" she asked quickly before he turned to leave. She misheard.
Another time she asked him out of curiosity, "How old are you?"
"64."
"Oh."

She assumed that his birth year was the same year as her parents, thinking that since her mother had just turned 64, that he must have been born in the same year. She was wrong. She misheard again. He actually said "65." Thus, she had assumed that he was one thing when he was, in actuality, another. She had thought he was her father's age, but he was actually less than a year older.

* * *

She told him so much about the pain she suffered through in a relationship void of love. She told him about the pain she suffered through with her family. He noted that she was quite rebellious. She thought he liked that about her. He was too, long ago. She thought he still was to some extent the original bad boy. They both had tensions in their family.

Wanting to be honest with him, as he was also her friend, she pulled up her pants' legs to show him the scars from March. They had healed enough that she only needed a cam boot on one leg. Thinking that he would be shocked or sympathetic, instead he took her bare foot and sucked her toes. She was surprised at the reaction, but she was also deeply into it. She thought his reaction was the best she could ever hope for.

* * *

She made a mistake though. They had a little less lust for a few minutes or hours because of what she did the next day. She knew what time he normally arrived; they usually arrived at the same time. When she saw his car pull up in the parking lot in the morning, she went out to greet him. He told her that that was one of the scariest things and that she was never to do that again. He said, "I'm angry, just give me a minute to calm down." He tried to think up excuses for it, work-related. She kept trying to persuade him that everything was okay. No one saw. And if they did, so what? It is not a crime. "I understand why you think that, but I do not want people to know. Office romances are tricky. The gossip mill is terrible." Oh, why did she have to try to persuade that stubborn ox to see her way so much more often than necessary?

* * *

Returning home was the worst. Ugh! Her boyfriend disgusted her. She did not want sex with him. Like a crazy person, she told her boyfriend how much she wanted to have sex with someone else. It is unavoidable. She had been touching herself more than usual for an exceeding number of hours in the preceding days. "I get tired of looking at your face," she told her boyfriend. For some reason, she could not stop telling the boyfriend how much she wanted another man. She wanted this other man more than anything, so much, so much. Threat thought that she finally understood how to play his game.

"Well, how about this? You can have sex with someone when I find a girl to have sex with. But it will not be with that man." He is too lazy to find another girl. He does not need to. What he does not need to do, he does not do, like find a job.

Thinking that she was trying to persuade him into bed, her boyfriend told her that she played a very hard game and proceeded to fuck her. She did not want it at the time, but she put up no fight.

CHAPTER 13

The End of Her Job

The eviction notice was on her apartment door, not because of anything she did. She knew who the culprit behind her pain and suffering was. She told him to leave. Go to a hotel room, she said.

When she got to her boyfriend's temporary living quarters after work, she threw a fit. Having put up with enough, she broke down. She threw a glass at the wall, watching it shatter and stain. She yelled at him and her parents on the phone. She yelled because this was not the life she wanted to lead. When she was finished, she curled up on the floor and cried like a baby, refusing to move, refusing to let go of the floor, the only thing in her life that was steady. He kept telling her to get up, but she would refuse.

The next day was Monday. She turned on her coworker.

"Can you check these boxes to make sure they have the right manuals in them?" her co-worker asked her.

She went to check each one to find that there was nothing wrong with them. She was angry for having done something with no purpose. It was too much like her everyday life at home.

Angrily she said, "I already checked them yesterday. Don't you see? I made a list. I thought you were supposed to help me, make my job a little easier. What are you doing?"

She did not think he knew how angry she was. Whenever she was angry, she compared herself to her father and remembered times when he would say, "I am not yelling. THIS IS YELLING!"

She remembered that a few days before her coworker had a relative who went to get psychiatric help because he tried to shoot himself. Her co-worker's reaction was, "Oh, he's just trying to get attention." If someone wants attention, there are so many other ways to get it, she thought. Being somewhat suicidal then herself, she was mad at the way he treated his relative. She wanted him to know what his relative thought of him.

"Don't give me bullshit. I have had enough bullshit," she said as she cut open boxes, as is her tasked job, inadvertently waving the scissors around in her hand since they were already there in her hand from opening boxes.

She could feel herself getting angrier and angrier over the smallest thing. It must have been the rush of blood to her head. Finally, she ran to the office secretary and told her, with damp eyes, that she needed to go home. She did not want to lose her job due to her temper. Leaving at the right time would have ensured that she wouldn't lose her job.

However, home was a hotel that day, because that was where her boyfriend was staying and that was where she was staying that night. However, her stuff was still in the apartment.

Not thinking that she made a scene, she got a surprise call from her employer. "You're fired." He told her. Leaving at the right time would have ensured that she wouldn't lose her job. Wrong! She was confused. She went home so that she would not be fired. She was doing all she could to make sure she was not fired. He told her that she was threatening her coworker with a weapon. Really? Was that so? Does anger automatically equal threats? However, there was nothing she could say. There was no one who could vouch for her. She just let things happen to her. She had gotten so used to having so much of her boyfriend's bad karma. His karma was the kind of karma that clung to her like a leech.

*　*　*

Flashback…

It wasn't the first time she had been fired. Another time he had threatened to leave her and let her walk home alone. They went to bed angry; they got up angry. She went to work angry, scaring her officemates half to death with her cuss words. When she left, he blocked her car in the parking lot to reason with her, saying that he was just trying to get her to exercise. The Human Resources Director noticed that he was bad news right away and gave him a trespass warrant.

*　*　*

Soon after, she sneaked out to Yue's place. "May I come in?" she asked timidly after having pulled up into the driveway. She explained what happened and all the turmoil happening in her life as they sat on stools in front of a clock. He listened without judging her.

"I like your skirt," he said. It was the first time he saw her wear a skirt since she normally dressed in jeans to work, an environment that is both casual and a little dirty.

Ring!

He picked up the phone, then with hand over the receiver, he told her, "My friend is coming over soon. You better leave."

CHAPTER 14

The Espionage

She was still interested in that man at work. She was sure he would not come to the wrong conclusions about her last days at work, listening to office gossip. Her boyfriend was visiting her that day instead of her visiting him. With her front facing the kitchen cupboards, her boyfriend approached her from the back. Her boyfriend reached into her back pocket and pulled out a condom. "Hello, what is this? I seem to find the weirdest things when I am not looking for them," he says. He peered at her curiously.

"That was when I was thinking about doing it with him, but we already talked about it, so I didn't do anything."
"I have been checking your phone."
"You have?" she squeaked, fear elevating.
"Will you please stop calling him?"
"Yes," she lied.

The next morning her boyfriend mutters, "Ok fine. Just do it. Then be done with it." Therefore, she proceeded to put on her coat.
"Where are you going?"
"You said to just do it."
"No, I did not."
"I'm pretty sure you did."
"I wouldn't say that" he insists.

"Can I at least call him to tell him goodbye?" she asked her boyfriend. "Fine but make it quick!"

She got her phone and closed the door to the bedroom.

Outside of the office, she called Yue and asked him what people in production were saying about her. He told her that they were saying she threatened her coworker with a razor. "That is bullshit," she said, not angry with the messenger.

With care and concern, as she talked to him within ear's reach of an angry man, he told her that he hoped things went well between her and her other man. It was a message that he would repeat in the future as he was unselfish and concerned more about her happiness.

"Why are you taking so long? It shouldn't take this long?" Her boyfriend yelled impatiently.
"I got to go," she said quickly into the phone and hung up.

* * *

When they had run out of money soon after she was fired from her job, they had to apply for food stamps. After they had returned home, he had the desire for her to buy groceries before they had even been approved for food stamps. That was the last straw.

She went "crazy" again with anger, throwing glasses again. Nevertheless, this time, she had murder in her eyes. She tried to push her boyfriend onto the broken shards. He, physically stronger than she, stood firm, while she cut her feet on the edges of the broken pieces. Her feet bled and bled and bled. At least 10 cc's. "Do you want my help?" he said, always willing to be kind and gentle after the worst of times.
"No." She did not trust him. Then the pain and the bleeding continued to get worse.
"Yes." she said after enough time had passed.

Her boyfriend wrapped her foot in a sock and put a bowl underneath her foot to collect the blood.

I can't do this anymore.

She told him to go to the hotel. She called his mother and told her to tell him goodbye.

She called the best people who would help her out.

In a couple of hours, all the belongings she could manage to move out of the apartment, she did, with some help. She was never able to find her makeup and music because that had been stolen earlier.

Then she told her helpers, her former hosts, that there is a man. In addition, she wanted to spend her last night there with him.

CHAPTER 15

May-to-Dec First Date

She told Yue that the next day she would be out of the state.

Starting from the beginning, she called him and told him that she was free.

He was not. Someone called, said they were coming over to visit.

Later, he called her to tell her the coast is clear. She told him that she was at a Mexican bar and asked him to come to her.

Dragging his feet, he said, "I'd rather stay home." Nevertheless, he gave it some thought. It is, after all a chance in a lifetime. She was so glad he made the decision he did.

She waited for what seemed like an eternity, afraid that he would not come, but he did show up. He ordered them some drinks and taught her how to play pool, telling her that she was a fast learner while he grabbed her butt from behind as he walked around her. He told her the way the pros play pool, the way he prefers to play pool. This is the only sport he likes, solitary things.

He said things like "If I were twenty years younger..."
"I like you the way you are," she interrupted him.

The song "Rockin' Robin" blasted from the speakers as they bopped to the lyrics.

They returned to his place, where she had decided to sleep the night before leaving on a jet plane to her parent's land. He turned his favorite music on. "Don't You Know" by Paul Hardcastle blared from the speakers, surrounding the world with euphoric atmosphere.

She complained about her ex briefly. "He was so stupid," she said.
"No shit," Yue replies.
She set down the rules for that night: "There will be no talk about the men in my life, neither my ex nor my father."
"I'm fine with that. Your kisses," he confessed, "are in the top five percent."
"Wow!" she said, amazed at her own talent.
"The first time we kissed was amazing."
She agreed.
"When you came down to the parts room and told me 'No more flirting,' I thought, where did that come from?" he said, "If I were younger, around your age, I would have been all over you. In the office that first day, you wanted to kiss me, right?"
"Yes."
"Did you notice what I did? I leaned in and then dodged so you could not kiss me. I wanted to kiss you too, but I was afraid about it being in the workplace. I did not want a sexual harassment lawsuit on my hands."
"Understood. Guess what. I'm a model." She decided to get into the industry after that day on the bus.
"I was a model too."
"Really?"
"A long time ago. It's too bad we can't go to the Renaissance Fair together."
"You like to go to Renaissance fairs? I love them! I didn't know they had them here."
"Oh yah!"
"So, what does being a Leo mean to you?"
"It means I'm very bold."

"My grandma was a Leo, but she was very different from you. She was modest. What makes her a Leo?"
"She must have masturbated every day."

!!!

Her mouth gaped open at his bold Leo-ness traits.

They talked a little more over a glass of water as she stared into his bright blue eyes. Then they proceeded, being more comfortable with each other, to walk to the bedroom and undress.
They had the most magnificent sex ever. She did something that she had not done for a long time, if ever, maybe only once before, and she realized why it started to feel like she was urinating in the bathtub since she confessed her interest in him. Her realization came when his realization came too, or should one say he just came. However, there was never anything "just" about it. It would be a scene she would replay in her head. He did too.

Instead of relaxing afterwards, they got up and moved about.

"I don't know if I want to have more sex with you or if I want to find out all I can about you," she said as she made herself sexily comfortable on his kitchen table.
"I agree," he told her.

He pointed out his dream house from a magazine article. It is all windows and wood. It is one story tall.

He pointed out other things as well, opening up the most on their first date before he would close up again. They felt so comfortable telling each other all their secrets, their dreams, their sadness, so much. He showed her his father's will.

"The bastard," he said, "did not leave anything for me. He left money for my daughters. It was because I divorced my ex-wife. It was very shameful."

There was not much more talk about his father. She did not know what to say.

"My grandma doesn't like Frank Sinatra," she said, "because he was a gambler."
"My parents didn't like Frank Sinatra either. Let's watch a movie."

They sat on the couch, with him to her left. He turned on the movie, but she did not want to spend her last night with him watching a movie. She told him so. He quickly agreed.

"So, tell me why your father..." he started.
"Remember the rule?" she reminded him.
"Okay, I won't mention it again."
"Do you mind if I ask what happened to your pointer finger?"
"Nothing, it's probably just from the repetitive motion of screwing things on vehicles." He got up to go to the kitchen area.
"Are you," he asks while he poured them drinks, "the type who goes from one relationship to another?"
"No," she said. That is just how it works out. I have not been single since I was in high school.
"When men show interest in you, play a little hard to get. Don't be easy."
"Okay."
"I thought about what it must have been like for you to be a Black Korean adoptee in an all-white family."
"Wow, most people don't even think about it."
"And another observation...most people when they start a new job are all 'Yessir,' but you are 'OK,'" He says, changing the subject and imitating her, somewhat acting a little ditzy. "You know, there are other women before you who got more attention than you in the workplace. You may think you have all the attention, but you didn't have the most."
"You are very, very sensitive," he continued in his observations of her.
"Is it obvious?"
"For sure," he said. It sounds like "fersher."
"Say that again," she said with an amusing smile.

"For sure," he said near the bed, "95% of the time, I can look at a person and describe his or her personality without even hearing them talk. Most folks who have lived awhile, and are somewhat astute, can do that exercise."
"There's a lot more to people than their personality. Everyone has stories to tell."
"Yup."
He sat down and beckoned her to sit on his knee. She asked intimate questions with long-term potential. "If we were to live together, do you think we could figure out the finances alright?" she asked, with her recent ex on her mind. He avoided the question; it is ridiculous. It is their first date.
"What is your contact information? What is your email address?"
He jotted it down on a piece of paper.

They made out again. She felt his skin. Even though he had patches of eczema on his joints, it did not cover his entire body as it did with her ex. It is such a strange thing that she had even gotten herself used to feeling second-best skin. To touch Yue's soft skin was such a pleasure to her.

After sex, therefore, meaning nothing, he told her that he loved her. She asked him when he knew that he loved her. He said when she turned around, and he watched her go, sounding rather lustful.

Thinking for a moment, not even a second, a light went off in her head as she realized that she loved him without needing him to love her. She said so as a reply to the next thing he said:

"If I were twenty years younger..."
"I love you the way you are. I love your eyes, your hair, your voice, your smell, your handwriting, everything about you. I love you."
Frightened, he said that she cannot love him.
She repeatedly said his name, to get his attention, trying to persuade him that it was true.
"Whaaa?" he complained in bed in reaction to hearing his name multiple times.

She repeated her sincere words, knowing for the first time in all honesty.

"Bullshit," he said in fear, perhaps he was the only one allowed to confess his love so early on.

"I'm very vulnerable."

"I know," he said, knowing all too well, but he was vulnerable too.

"Time"
At first,
you were a nice smile
to smile back at a little too long.
At first,
you were an option,
a very good choice.
At first,
you were a way to salvage
my lost dreams,
you were a way to revitalize me.
Now,
I see you as a lighthouse,
steady and bearing light.
Now,
I see you as real,
more real than anyone else.
Now,
I am ready to hang my
recovered dreams
on the impossible,
on a romantic wish.
Later,
my dreams will become
a daily, fulfilling stroll,
not comparable to
singularity and loneliness.
Later,
we will match our
jigsaw pieces from a past life.

Later,
we will recall all our firsts.
Love should be easy.
It was never supposed to be
hard.
Only cocks are meant to be hard.
Love was not supposed to be painful
even when it hurts so good.
Love is peaceful,
not stressful.
It is thoughtful,
but not full of worry,
not hair-pulling.
Love is loyal,
not clingy, not leeching.
Love is not the same as passion.
Passion fuels anger and hate.
No,
what I have for you is peace.
I have learned that war is not peace,
nor do they go together.
Peace is good alone
and love goes with peace.
How could I know so suddenly
that I have found what I want?
People who do not know what they
are looking for never find it.
But I found peace.
And I found you.

* * *

The next morning, she found that her car would not start.

Yue drove her to the nearest hotel so she could catch a taxi to the airport.

He told her later that he and his coworker found out there was sugar, soap, or something in the gas tank.

It may have been poured into her car when they were at the bar or maybe before when she went to her apartment for the last time.

She signed the lease of the car over to his friend, and her coworker, who discovered the problem with the gas tank. It was a good thing he collected cars.

CHAPTER 16

Departure, Arrival into Long-Distance Land

Up in the air, she talked to the only man who had ever loved her the most the next day, even more than Yue; the man who came to rescue a damsel in distress. She made it clear that they were not hooking back up. He understood. They talked sincerely then and over time about boundaries and love: the meaning of love, how to know when you are in love, and other things about love. He never brought up the topic of unrequited love.

When she returned home, where her parents moved to in Maryland, her parents would not let her go, smothering her with kisses and hugs, thankful that their prayers were answered. It was such a dramatically different reaction from before, when she chose to cleave to a young man.

* * *

When she returned home, Yue told her that "our night together could not have been more magical." Magical. That was a word they used often to describe how they felt. Magical is how she continued to see it. It was a miracle. He ended with "let's stay in touch" to which she told him that "stay in touch" sounded too much like a "goodbye" and that they would stay in touch as soon as possible, as often as possible.

Around this time, they tried various lengths of email letters to each other until they found what worked for them.

"Did I ever tell you that you are a horrible conversationalist via email?" she ask, perturbed.
"Oh yah! However, you are a writer. I tend to keep my verbosity to a minimum. After a few cocktails, I can talk a mile a minute."

Therefore, she tried again.

"Now you have it! Little sentences," he said.

One time later, she found a boy who was interested in dating her. He wrote longer emails and was more artistic with the words he chose, but on the first date with him, she knew that there were no sparks. Whatsoever.

* * *

They shared their literal dreams with each other over the phone. Hers involved reading the Kama Sutra. His dream he could not fully remember. All he knew was that it was "racy."

* * *

They sent each other pictures of themselves so that they had each other to gaze upon whenever they wanted.

* * *

May 13th, two days before her Mom's birthday, she told him via email that she did not want to scare him off. He told her, "You are not scaring me away." She asked him in the same email more about him. He told her he used to own a bar, like her friend's parents, back in the seventies before disco and country became more popular. He controlled the music. He got the girls (and made them cry, she bet).

* * *

May 19th, he told her again how beautiful she was, as she introduced him to her modeling portfolio. She never tired of these things, these compliments, flattery.

* * *

Two whole weeks after they had seen each other, he confessed in days back-to-back that he still fantasized about them making out at work or at his place.

* * *

On the 23rd, her dog died, and she told two people the same news. Her friend responded in a way that she did not like; he did not respond to any feelings she had about her aged dog, choosing instead to talk about himself. They are no longer friends. However, her new boyfriend responded to her with empathy, telling her how sad he was when his dog had died.

"If my living situation were such (a proper house and a yard), I would most certainly get another dog," He told her, "Have always thought that raising a kitten and a puppy together would bring a fair amount of joy." Since then, she would fantasize about bringing him a dog and cat for which they would share responsibilities.

"What breed was the last dog you owned? I agree that it would be cute to raise a puppy with a kitten."

"Well, he and his brother were cuties. . . A mix of a Cavalier King Charles Spaniel, Poodle, and a good mix of a larger dog, like maybe a Collie or some other larger dog."

"That would be interesting if your past dog had some Collie in him since my past dogs were akin to Collies; they were Shetland Sheepdogs."

"He was more like a large Cocker Spaniel. He had big floppy ears. I was so sad when he died."

* * *

At the end of May, she had read a book he recommended to her from when they were at work. "You can stand on your own with the help of friends and family. The book Passages will explain all that anyway. You are due to go through a passage and/or you may already be experiencing it…" she always took his recommendations seriously, even if he recommended more than what she could buy at once. Anyways, so she read this book about the different stages of life by age. She shared with him excerpts from the book. He told her how he does not know what to expect from the retirement stage of life. From that book, she came up with the belief that at similar ages, men and women are at different mental stages that do not coincide very well with the other person in a relationship. It brought her hope, as most things did where their relationship was concerned, such as Chinese horoscopes, that the difference in age actually made them more compatible. Maybe the Chinese horoscope was created because age-gap relationships were more common in China.

* * *

He told her also that "writing for him, has always been akin to pulling teeth." However, it takes email to help a long-distance relationship work. She was astonished at his desire to write emails to her every day. He must really like me! she thought. He even, at one point, told her that he was not good at phone conversations, to which she again thought, He must really like me!

* * *

In some emails to him, she would spout out the thoughts churning in her mind as her life was changing. She would talk about how she thought that long-distance actually was best for both of them, how they had their independence, how they could not control each other, and how they could not be caretakers for each other. In addition, the time difference worked well for them. He got to go to bed when he wanted to, and she got to go to bed when she wanted to. He agreed on all points entirely. They enjoyed sharing deep thoughts together.

* * *

It was in May that they planned a wonderful time together. They had hoped it would be in July or August, but it happened to occur in September.

* * *

Flirting over the Net, she told him how she would love to be his birthday present even though it was not even until July. "You have no idea how I would love that!" he said joyfully.

* * *

"Specimen of Love"
Any sort of doubt
is an implant in the head
based on what has been said
about the past,
based on what I said
in the heat of unforgiving anger.
By letting go of a dream,
By doubting my own reasonable intuition,
others have domain
and more power.
When I lost control of everything
and did not understand anything,
my friends and family took me
and they held my hand with their wings.
All they can see is what
the outside will show
because they were not there for me

then.
By submitting myself to a counselor,
I concede my judgment to someone else
who will preside
and tell me when I am healthy,
though I can take care of myself.
Everyone doubts what I know,
but they do not doubt what I have been through.
The love I profess, that I know,
does not convince
the people who were not there for me
then.
It does not even convince the subject of my love,
who deems my love lust.
Love is a learning experience, and I was the only one
to experience it. But my experiences have made me "crazy."
I have been put in a petri dish,
and now I am just a specimen of love.

Her counselor, the one she went to so that she could figure out what went wrong with her relationship before Yue, told her that she should not get involved with anyone so soon after leaving an abusive relationship. She told Yue, and he agreed with her (even though anything she had told Perez about what her counselor said he disagreed with):

"Your counselor is correct. You are on a path of discovery, that being, finding out who you are. You know some things; however, you will be learning how cool a person you are, and all the things that you are capable of (that, sometimes takes a number of years. Knowing who you are opens doors to many possibilities for yourself! Confidence and a belief in yourself can be, and are, quite rewarding.

You are a writer, a teller of tales. You are a person who can translate pedestrian thoughts and actions into a cognitive and sometimes, fun narrative. I believe, once you have gained some knowledge of those things, mentioned above, your spirits will soar at times, and you will accomplish good and noble endeavors. For you... the future is bright!"

* * *

She asked him about what he planned to do for retirement. She asked, "What do you want to do aside from a part-time job?"

"Make love to you!"

"You're so sweet! However, I do not want to be the reason for you to change your plans unless you just really, really want to."

"The future is not for us to predict."

* * *

She told him that what she loved about him was how he complimented her with sincerity.

"It's you girl, it's you!" he says.

* * *

"I'm a horrible cook!" she told him.
"Given the opportunity, I can help…"
"Thanks. How different times are now! The man teaches the woman to cook."
"And cook we will!"
"We should dance too"
"We should! Dancing can be a very personal expression."

* * *

Most everything in May occurred via email. They used separate emails for clean conversations and dirty conversations. They had a mind connection, baby.

CHAPTER 17

June

Threat sat upright. Then, tired of sitting, he stood, as if rising from the ashes. He paced back and forth. He was not grateful for the mess she left him in, he was not grateful to clean up that mess, but he was glad to get her off his mind a few minutes in a day. It was temporary though, for his thoughts returned to her and her deceit, her betrayal. Every girlfriend he ever had had left him for another man. He could not figure out why. He did not think of himself as a bad person, yet bad things befell him. He paced and paced, a prisoner of his own karma, or bad choices. He paced, disabled with the inability to understand the world around him, and the people around him. He was destined to live in a desert, no matter how much snow would lay around him in the winter months. His life was barren. All he could hope for was a mirage.

* * *

She found an apartment, with her parents as the guarantors.

"When I finally move into my new apartment, expect a call from me. I will have complete privacy."

"You're on. I'll meet you in bed," he emailed. They did something the day she moved into her apartment that he told her was the most exciting thing since they departed from each other. They made love on the phone. "I'm so massive!" he told her, riling her up. He told her so many sweet things. She could not even hear him half the time because he was talking so low. His voice was so sexy though that she never bothered to tell him she did not hear him because she understood his passion enough to make her cum. She continued to fall in love with his voice like it was the first time.

* * *

She was still looking for a job. He told her that he gave her "a super job recommendation. Do not remember the company, but it was an eager-beaver type who interviewed me. Will be in/or near Baltimore Sunday evening. I will be dropping the trucks off at the Baltimore port Monday morning, then flying back the same day. So close..." His recommendation did not help her get the job, but she was so happy, nevertheless. Gaithersburg was less than an hour away, but it was also a workday.

He came over June 7th. He said on his business trip to Maryland that he was "so close." Then he called her when she was at dinner with her parents and left her a voicemail: "You sound busy. I am a few minutes from your place. Anyways [with the inflection on "anyways"], call me back." she asked if her parents could drive her back home, saying that a friend wanted to hang out with her. She waited all night in the lobby. She kept his voicemail message saved as long as her phone would allow, just so she could hear his voice. When she heard from him again, he told her that his phone had not been working and that it was too late to come over. She regretted that they were not able to see each other that day. She was so frustrated, sexually, and emotionally. So was he.

"I read some of Passages while I was waiting patiently for your phone to come back on," she stated. She specifically read the part about sex at an older age. She asked, "Do you think that you'll stay at the same place next time you are sent to the Baltimore port? That would be lucky."
"We'll keep our fingers crossed. Next time, I will plan... Will do taxi. However, I think I will leave on Tuesday, for somewhere else."

"Tuesday?! They hardly give you a break."

"That's OK... Racking up the hours... Anything over forty goes into vacation days. I am on the 'end of the road trail' as far as this company goes... I will work no more than one more year... I can hear the swan song already."

"Beautiful song."

"Then it's off to somewhere where it is warm all the time..."

(He also told her later that he did not want to move now because he did not want to lose money on his house.)

There would be other times. He would be going to the port for his job in the future. They did not lose hope and continued to plan for the next time. She got excited, telling him about the restaurants in the area. "Cost is not a factor," he said, even though it was. He told her, "Do you think we will have food on the brain when we meet?"

* * *

She declared their official start date as April 20th, even though it was not because she could not remember exactly. He concurred.

* * *

"Heard you had some wild weather near your home a few days ago. Correct?"

"Yesterday: My parents left at 4PM for an Orioles game, which, of course, never happened. My aunt picked me up to see my choral director's 20th anniversary concert. First, we went out to eat. My aunt showed me her neighbor's house. A tree crashed through the master bedroom. Unfortunately, the house is leased. Many car accidents occurred due to traffic lights being out. She drove her where there were few traffic lights to a restaurant. Right after they got in, twelve people lined up right behind us, with the line going out the door. Everyone was thinking the same thing. During the early middle of the concert, everyone in the auditorium was asked to do a 15-minute tornado drill in the halls. My former high school looks horrible because it is overcrowded (lockers cover murals that were made when I was there, and the entire front of the building is hidden by trailers). Also, there is tons of construction. We return to the concert at 8:15PM."

"Today: Past a roadblock, one could see a huge tree that fell on top of the electrical lines. Many trees had fallen elsewhere, such as on people's decks and fences. People on the radio claimed that power would come back to the area 10PM today and that thousands in my area were affected. I even heard that it affected people as far as Ohio, since that's where the tornado came from."
"Holy shit!"

* * *

He told her that he missed her. He did not say how much. That would be unnecessary.

* * *

She looked up his horoscope. She was thrilled. They were perfectly matched using both horoscopes: Western and Chinese. The horoscopes were too good to be true. Much to her dismay, she discovered that she was using the wrong date when he mentioned his age another time.

"I have to confront you about something. What year were you born? I specifically remember that you said '44. However, that cannot be since my dad was born in that year and is turning 64. I admit that math is not my strong suit, but this just does not make sense. What is going on?"
"Born in '43."
"Do you remember saying '44? I am sure because I wrote it down. I do not like realizing that what I have been thinking all along is inaccurate."
"Maybe I was trying to be a year younger."
"Never mind. Just forget about it. I think I figured out what was up. When we started dating, my mom had just turned 64 and when you said you were the same age, I probably just applied the same year to you. I apologize for the accusation and confusion. It was my mistake."
"It happens allll the time," he emailed, forgivingly.

"I'm glad that you're cool about it. That's embarrassing."

The horoscope results the second time were not as cheerful. Yet, she consoled herself that the wrong date was not too far off. What it said before sounded so accurate. The only thing that stayed the same was blood type. At least in that they were compatible.

* * *

Yue told her how much he thought of her. He told her how often he looked at her picture and fantasized. "There are times," he said, "when you take my breath away." One time when she was fearful that he would leave, as he said he would, since it is a temporary relationship and all, he told her, "Take comfort in the fact that I think about you all the time."

* * *

They always loved emailing each other and getting a reply back soon ("Are you online right now? I love it when we're online at the same time"). They kept track of when each other was on the computer. Sometimes they were not at the computer at the same time. They would wait up for each other, hoping. In addition, they would tell each other, out of courtesy, when the day's email session would end. They had many ways of saying "goodnight."

Sometimes he would wonder if she were there, leaving emails of "Are you home?"

Sometimes she would get worried if he were not there. One time she called, and he was not there. "Are you at home? I have a weird feeling that something has changed. Am I wrong?"
"Noooo, not that I know of.... I see you called last night.... I was asleep. The phone was in the living room. I went to bed early, as I have a full day today. Dentist, Social Security, then off to work, then go home, eat, go to my hair cutting friend, back home and pack and prepare for the next truck-driving trip. Have a full plate this week as well as next. I

will write a little more tonight and try to give you a call." She was glad that he gave her a rundown of his day. It showed her respect.

* * *

Finally, her hair grew longer. Her freedom to not shave... she was so happy to be her again. He was so happy too, that she was happy.

* * *

"Do you like hot weather?" Yue asked.
"Yes."
"I am looking forward to moving to a warmer climate. You have no idea how I hate living here. I hate cold weather. Am a warm and humid kind of guy. I am a hot guy."
"Yes, you are."

Stunned silence.

"You are so cool," he says, doing that thing he does with his voice when he is bashful.

* * *

She made a suggestion of something she wanted to do with him: shower together. "How do you like the idea of showering together?" she asked curiously.
"I love it!" he said.

It was one of their favorite activities after that. Both of them would fantasize about each other whenever they took their daily showers. Whenever she heard the rain, she would always think about how she wanted to make love to him in the rain.

* * *

She asked him to send her some music, thinking he would attach one or two of his favorite songs in an email. He sent her about 12-14 CDs and good speakers so that she could hear the music well. It took her a while to figure out how to turn the volume up and down. A few days after her entertainment system was set up, her father asked her where she got it. "A friend," she said in a half-truth. The music came later. It was mostly smooth jazz and blues, music he listened to as a teenager, punctuated with some techno, the kind that was not too fast. She normally had never taken much to slow music, but ah! Love makes one's interests change sometimes, kinda like those moments when she is honestly interested in football. However, she wondered if a disinterest in each other's music could be a deciding factor. Then she tried not to think like that. The sounds were unique, like none she had ever heard in pop music. They were instrumental mostly, not like the lyrical, melodic music she listened to so that she could sing along. She copied his music to her iTunes and brought the music to work so she could listen to it every day. She carefully tried to send him some music of hers that she thought sounded like his. She had a feeling that he did not care for it. He never told her in detail what he thought except that he did not like fast-paced beats anymore; he was very different from Perez. Some of the music CDs she gave him did not work, of course they were the ones she wanted him to hear the most: the music she was sure he had never heard, not the pop music. He saved them for sentimental reasons.

* * *

She showed a trusted friend his picture. He told her that he looked like a cross between Mark Twain and George Carlin. Yue said that he had been told that before. He sent her a picture from when he was being compared to Albert Einstein—the way he looks after a wild session of sex, she thought with a grin.

* * *

"There was a period in my life (early teens to mid-teens), when I thought living in a large city would be cool."
"I thought so too, that's why I started out near Notre Dame. Then I realized that I prefer suburbs that are near cities."

"I, too, have become a suburban denizen."
"Too much crime in the cities. It's harder to trust city people."
"Too busy for me…"

* * *

After noticing his habit of always paying for her meals, she made sure that Yue understood that she was not looking for a sugar daddy. She was no gold-digger, even if she did like the song by Kanye West. From what she had been through, she would not wish that on anybody. He understood.

* * *

Another time, she did not remember what they were talking about, he said, teasingly, "Just fucking with you."
"Don't fuck with me," she replied coyly, "just fuck me."
"My God woman, how I wish it were so," he said.

* * *

She talked to him about Halloween costumes. She told him what she loved to hear. He told her that he preferred her "especially, sans costume." She told him that she did not have a picture of herself dressed up in the things she liked to wear for Halloween. "Can wait," was his reply. Can you, can you wait? she wondered. Can you wait for me? I will wait for you.

* * *

Every now and then he would say something that disturbed her a little, such as the time when he said, "Sometimes I think about you romantically and have to catch myself."
"Why?" she asked, "feel free to think of me romantically anytime."

* * *

When Father's Day rolled around, he was disappointed not to hear from his daughters (they probably forgot), but she called. That was something. "No word from the kids... However, I received a message from the oldest this AM. I'll pass it on to you." He forgot to pass along her message. She also noted that he referred to his daughters as "kids" though they were older than her. That was a little awkward.

"Father's Day is not like Mother's Day," she told him.

* * *

She worried about him. She wanted him not to worry so much about age like other people. He had so much more life to live. It would be a shame for him to think of himself as older than he was. She never got a response to this email. She was not surprised:

"In terms of age, I feel that growing older should not be an embarrassment or something undesirable. In fact, on the front of the Washington Post Style section today is a man who wrote his first novel at the age of 88. If anything, I think that now is the best time to grow older, since 60 is the new 40 and so on. I guess that makes me a newborn. J/k. I have always been taught to be honest when asked about one's age and never to pluck gray hairs. People might say that I should find someone to grow old with, but when you age, I age, and when I age, you age. So, what if we are not the same age? So, what if you might (no offense), be closer to death? I think that would just enhance the feeling of loving as if tomorrow were your last, n'est-ce pas? I like the age difference also because I am a curious person. I love to hear true life stories, and the more you have lived the more you have to tell. One of the things my family always told me about my Black exes was that they were not my intellectual equals. I took that to mean that my family was being racist, which created animosity toward them for ages it seems, but it finally was explained to me that what they meant was that I have a natural curiosity about life, and the men I had dated before did not. Or, more generally, I love to learn, and I love to live."

* * *

Yue and Zarah talked about things to do in the future, vacations they could take.

"Williamsburg, VA is beautiful in the fall... I was there once for a first snowfall... The place was enchanting..." So, they decided on Williamsburg in November. He used to live on the East Coast at Ocean City, MD. He has lived all over, just like her. She also kept asking if he wanted to go camping in October to meet her friends, but he said that he had had enough sleeping on the ground from the Air Force.

"Fill in the blanks: We will go camping as long as the forecast says that the temperature will be _____ or above. Otherwise, we'll find something else to do," she wrote.

"When do you propose this? I am not a camper. Hate sleeping on the ground. Had enough of that in the military." She was disappointed; her twenty- to forty-something friends are openminded. They would have liked him.

After some thought, flip-flopping somewhat, he said, "70 Degrees."

* * *

"Do you tend to go for things off the beaten path?" she asked.
"Absolutely! I am not a touristy kind of person. I am a side street sort of person."

* * *

They would also share their opinions of politics and computers. They both hated Windows Vista. They talked about news: Ms. Rhee in DC, taxes, Russia, and how the media spins the truth. Politics was quite a hot topic. They spoke like true Democrats, even though she had never been able to call herself one, feeling that to do so would betray her father. However, every time she wanted to ask serious questions and peer a little more into him, he would always tell her that such discussions were to be saved for face-to-face. He would never tell her that much about his daughters or his estranged younger brother. He never opened up to her the way they did on their first date. Maybe because he thought he would never hear from her again. However, you know, she did not think they ever talked about the things when they were face-to-face that she had brought up as questions to him before. Because she just did not remember what she had asked him. Perhaps that was his idea all along.

* * *

Ring! Ring! Ring!
"Hello," she answered.
"Is this sending the wrong message?" said a voice, which she did not recognize.
"Message? Voicemail? I haven't checked my voicemail today."
"No, I said, 'Is this sending the wrong message?'"
Pause. All of a sudden, a tidal rush of feeling overcame them both, deep like the ocean water.
"Is this you?"
"Yes. I'm sorry about everything."
"Me too. I forgive you. It was a bad way to have left. We both behaved badly."

The next day she emailed him his resume, which she updated.

Perez and Zarah continued to wish that they were in each other's presence (secretly), though she knew the good points of them being apart. What else was one to wish, being in a long-distance relationship, being apart from sex too often, letting one's mind stray from time to time to the past? She did not know if he did, but she did not just wish; she prayed. Fervently did she pray. What she prayed for was to know true love. She never knew how she would learn it and who would teach it to her. Would they both teach her how to love?

"Vase"
I am the porcelain vase,
or the celadon vase,

that broke when you threw
your own fears
and crushed me underfoot.
I am the dream you have
as you wake to the alarm.
I will be there when
you are ready for me,
even if that means
after death.
I will return when you
can give me what I give you.
I'll return,
O ye of little faith,
when there are no obstacles,
because I am a believer.
I'll return when you
take a summary
of your life
and feel like you have lost
something besides your keys.
You may never believe
in the depth of my soul,
but someone out there
believes in you
even when you have nothing
to show, even when you
do not believe in your
own self-worth.
I'll return when
I have put myself back together
with a durable glue.

CHAPTER 18

July

She warned Yue of weather conditions before she knew he would be heading out to see her. She told him to be careful. "I most soitenly will!!!" he says lively.

* * *

She asked him to tell her about his education. His first degrees were in Political Science and Economics. He got two more degrees on the GI Bill: Business and Construction Management. He went to Notre Dame University when he was still a Chinese citizen. She majored in English at Notre Dame.

* * *

She sweetened him with adjectives when she said goodnight or just because. He smiled with increased font size. "You have been hanging around the Thesaurus shop too long. But I love it," he told her flattered.

* * *

They shared their fantasies with each other while others lay deep inside their heads, or at least in hers. In her imagination, they had done

everything together. She wondered at times when she could bring up anal, even though she wasn't all that into it; it was a remnant from the past. They talked about "love in an elevator." She imagined that they were talking about an elevator that went up, but never went down. They told each other all the memories they had planned to make: "I hope to give you sweet new memories soon."
"Delicious ones…"
"So delicious that they melt in your mouth."
"Ahhhh, a literate description…"

At the end of July, they used their imaginations over the phone. She soaked up his imagination, and it went straight for her crotch. He admitted to her that the day after their lustful event that he forgot to take off her thong in his dialogue.

* * *

"Timing can be everything!" Yue exclaimed at one point. She felt that their timing was both perfect and imperfect.
"Wish there were more of it…more time to be together, more time to get things done, more time on the weekends…"
"Yup. Just living a little closer would help. But for now, it is OK. Getting your feet on the ground is high priority."
"Thanks sugar. I cannot tell you how much I wish you were here in my arms and in my bed. However, we are both strong and independent people. Things happen for a reason. In addition, things change. We have both been changing, whether or not it's partly due to being in this relationship."
"Yes ma'am!"

* * *

Hopeful, she tried her hand at tarot cards, wishing to find something delightful. She got annoyed though that she kept getting the same results. She often would get the Wheel of Fortune card somewhere in the middle. As for the result, the future prediction, it kept turning out to be the same: an upside down Three of Swords, indicating heartbreak.

She tried a different tactic. She called up a psychic. The psychic told her not to return to her ex now, but that they would have a good relationship in a few years. Things were not looking so good for Yue.

"Please Ask Jesus How I Am"
All day long
I sit
paralyzed.
My face freezes
into a melancholic glare,
glazed with curiosity
as I try to
decipher tea leaves,
horoscopes, I-Ching,
just to know how you are.
I find ways
to get close to you
daily
so that I do not lose
sight
of what can be.
I have to have
so much faith.
I have to believe
that you think of me.
I made the decision
to be stable
and unrelenting.
Jesus will know
how to let you know
that I am thinking of you
without end.

* * *

Zarah and Yue talked about serious things again, identity this time rather than the meaning of love. "Have given this some thought," he emails in reply, "One may never know totally one's self. However, one learns one's boundaries. There may be some things that one does not even wish to bring to the fore in one's thoughts. It is not necessary. Just be yourself, and usually all turns out well."

* * *

Ring! Ring!
"Hello." It was that familiar/unfamiliar voice again.
"Hey."
"What's up?"
"I saw something that reminded me of you the other day. I felt like calling."
"That's nice."
"I talk about you a lot."
"I dream about you."
"I know you better than anyone else. You are just like me. We should be together."
"You don't know me. If you love me, you have a funny way of showing it."

She told herself that she did not leave him, that she just moved to have a physical boundary. The next day she found a good deal on a computer and had it shipped to him.

CHAPTER 19

Second Date

As they planned their second outing, they threw around the idea of going to Wolf Trap. Out of all her ideas, he liked that one best. It was outdoors. "As long as I can touch you..." he emailed. However, the time he actually came was not the time of the event they wanted to see. No worries. No money was spent.

"OK... Here is the tentative schedule... My plan would be to arrive Monday morning, rent a car about noon, and then drive to you. I probably will not arrive at your place until sometime after two... Stay the night of the 16th, have the next full day (I know it is a weekday), stay the evening of the 17th, then leave in the morning for the airport when you go to work on Wednesday and catch a return flight at about noon..."

He arrived just as she was walking up to her apartment in a tailored suit. She went inside to get him a parking pass, then waited for him by her back door. Within 30 seconds to a minute, they were undressed and wild. She made the most interesting of noises: purrs, growls, and screams. Her neck moved her ecstatic head in many directions while her legs were pulled up to her chest. Every time he pulled out, teasing her, she would go crazy from being teased, moaning, yelling, screaming. She thinks she remembered her ecstasy at that moment more than she remembered his. It went by so fast she could barely remember all the details. She just remembered that they had the most amazing sex. It was even better than their first date. Well, no. It was just different.

After sex, she noticed that his chest hair was white, and his leg hair was Black. She loved learning these little things. She loved to map his body in her mind. She remembered all his many textures. She will never forget. They finally got up.

They spent time trying out different stores, like Target and Giant, looking for something to bring to the pool. He bought Dove Pro Age soap. "You should try this stuff," he said. In the parking lot of one of the stores, he noticed a car that resembled his car back home and walked around it curiously noting the year of the car.

They mixed up some Absolut vodka and Ocean Spray cranberry juice in some cheap tumblers and added canned beer to the cooler they bought. The Dewar's was for later. They collected their pool supplies, applied sun lotion (helping each other, of course), put on their bathing suits, and went to the pool. They held hands, lucky to be able to do so.

The pool was closed on Mondays.

Still wanting to feel the summer breeze, they laid out their beach towels on a bench. He pulled out his iPod and played his favorite tunes.

"This apartment used to be a nice place," he observed, "Yep. A long time ago."
"Do you like architecture?"
"Yes."
"I used to want to be an architect when I was studying geometry in school," she said. Moving the conversation on, she said, "That movie you recommended to me... I am going to wait to see it. I do not really like Ernest Hemingway."
"Why?"
"He is a womanizer."

Yue laughs, "I am womanizer. That is not a good reason for not liking him."

They enjoyed the moment, not knowing how long it will last. They did not have to say anything to each other.

They spent a lot of time outside. That is what he preferred. Ambiance. And cigarettes—Marlboro Lights. He preferred to bask in Vitamin D rather than in the breeze of the A/C. He preferred anything that is very different from what makes his town famous. She racked her brain for outdoor dining facilities. She never gave the thought to eating outdoors. He did not want to eat Mexican, but he suggested seafood. Aha! She did not know if there was outdoor dining there, but she knew where to find a seafood restaurant. She printed out the directions on Mapquest, and they went there in his bright blue rental car. Lo and behold, they could sit outside by the parking lot.

They looked at the menu and chose oysters and scallops.

"I have never tried oysters," she said, proudly and bravely flaunting her willingness to try new things as she did on their first date. She delighted in the exquisite salty, buttery, slippery taste of the oysters. First times are always fun.

He pointed out a lady behind them who looked a lot like Judi Dench.

"She does look a lot like her, doesn't she?" she said.

They held hands and their knees touched. He joked a little when the waitress came around. He told Zarah that he noticed Asian women looking at her, wondering why she was with a man like him. She was amused.

Before they got up to leave, they were offered a free cookie. Amelie found that she had some difficulties with nutrition because if she was offered free food, which was usually full of carbohydrates, that she would take it every time. This was as a result of living through financially hard times with Threat; she was always afraid that something catastrophic would happen and that she would not be able to afford another meal.

He had trouble driving back because he was in an unfamiliar place.

They returned home to make passionate love. As she was on top of him, he said, "What are you doing to me?" she felt the thud as he hit the floor of Falling in Love.
"I feel very strongly about you," she said.
"I am starting to feel the same way."
The next day, they had breakfast outside at a place he found while he was driving to her place.

They went back to her apartment to collect their pool supplies like the night before and headed out from her apartment, with their flip-flops flapping at our ankles.

As they settled under a table shaded by an umbrella (her skin is too creamy, not suitable for tans), they squinted despite the shade.

He played their song: "Lost Without You" by Robin Thicke and tapped along to the beat of the cymbals. She used to hate that song, but now it is what she thinks of when she thinks of Yue. When he thought about her, other songs he thought of were "The Sky" and "Someone Else's Eyes" by Robin Thicke. He told her that he would play those three songs repeatedly for hours, lost in dreaminess.

"I used to have long hair," he told her.
"I can see that" she said as she envisioned him with biker hair.
"It's amazing how that helps pick up girls." She nodded.
"Were you a cute kid?" He asked.
"Yes, I was."
"I bet you were!"
"So, tell me a little about your ex."
"That was also an age-gap, but it was not quite as large."
"What was the gap?"

"We were less than 30 years apart."

"Hmm."

"She was a pumper," he said referring to her in bed, "She was married then divorced her husband to marry someone else who worked where she worked. He was not very impressive. She said that I sexually harassed her after we broke up, which was complete bullshit. Girls who are attracted to older men tend to be a little twisted."

"Am I?"

"Yes, a bit."

"I'm not monogamous," she said recalling that she cheated on her ex to be with her current partner.

"Nor am I, but if I found the right person I would be. It is an issue of respect."

"Have you ever been in love?"

"I have been in love a handful of times...three...maybe five times," he said.

"So, you say you've been in love several times. Who were they with? Your ex-wife?"

"No, I never loved her. In fact, maybe I have never been in love." That was when she realized how much he changed his mind. Therefore, it gave her hope every time he would push her away "for her own good."

"Sex is easily confused with love," he said.

"But" he added, "love can sometimes be confused with sex."

"What do you think about when you think about us?"

"Actually, I have been reading various accounts about near death experiences and the afterlife." Uh...how does that answer my question?

"Do I make you feel older?"

"No. You make me feel like I am fifty years old."

"What do you think about me?"

"I see you as worldly, but unsophisticated. No offense, but you are too trusting." That was my downfall, certainly.

"So where do you see us going?" she asked to his squinting eyes, expecting an answer she would not receive.

"I do not see us going anywhere. The money issue is huge. You need to stay where you are and establish yourself."

"I was thinking, I could be with you for five years. I know I can last that long in a relationship. I cannot promise anything past that."

"In five years, I'll be about 70." God, how she hated how he repeated that to her so often after this day.

"So?"

"You'll find someone else or I'll find someone else. There is no long-term potential. In addition, money is a big issue. I will be retiring soon. I do not have a retirement account and am living off social security. I cannot afford to live in the states. You do not have money either. It would be unfair to you. Let's just enjoy ourselves and have fun."

"A comment I have to make about the 'being unfair' comment you made: If you want to be fair to me, then do what you can to keep yourself living longer, meaning laugh more and smoke less and eat antioxidants," she said. "God, I love the sound of your laughter..." she added.

"Am trying..."

"Truth Seeker"
When you lie
to yourself,
You lie
to me.
You lead me on
so that you can take,
take back my goals, dreams,
some at least.
When you
flip-flop
like a politician
waving in the breeze,
when you do not dig deep,
when you do not know
what you are feeling,
when you cannot explain to me,
what is in your heart,
then I wonder
if I will ever be able
to figure you out.
Do not be my lover,

just to be my friend.
Do not test the waters
to see if it is a boiling temp.
Do not wear me out
with your constant lies
to yourself,
Do not hurt me
and make me fear.
I loathe your fear and guilt.
I hate waiting.
But I love you.
I will wait for you to be
exorcized of guilt,
that which cannot let a relationship
survive—
I will survive
to see you survive.

They gathered up their supplies and went back to the apartment. She told him to open his birthday presents. She got him his favorite movie, West Side Story, on DVD and a Vince Flynn books-on-tape. He was so pleased, like she could read his mind. He gave her a kiss. They both loved musicals. At some point, she wanted to watch Singing in the Rain with him.

They watched a bit of West Side Story. She pointed out that the wallflowers at the dance were all wearing green.

"Wow! I never noticed that. You're right," he said. She thought he noted his own appreciation of their differences in how they see things.

Throughout several points in the day, they would just start making out, whether it was on the couch or in her bed. She pointed out to him that her bedsheets just happened to be his favorite color.

When they took a break to go to the bathroom, he said to her, "I will never understand this relationship, but I'm going along with it."

After much sex, "I'm tired. You have worn me out. I have used muscles I have not used before in a while. I am a broken man," he told her. They rested a while. She enjoyed it when he lay on top of her.

They ate out again, roaming around, not knowing what they would find. They found a Vietnamese bar. It was too noisy. The music was like nails on a chalkboard to him. He could not stand to be there one minute. They went to the Korean restaurant next door.

"This place used to be a nice place," he observed. "It probably used to be a steakhouse. This is a family-owned business. I wonder how long they have had it."

He walked up to the bar and asked the lady behind the bar what they had. He ordered her a gin and vodka. It was good. She had never had one before. He asked the woman behind the bar how long they had been in business. Not that long.

He looked at the foreign menu, not sure what to get.

"We can still get pizza instead. We have only ordered drinks," she said. "We could," he said thinking, "No, that is okay."

After she finished eating a spicy dish, the waitress brought another. He ate it before she could warn him of how spicy it was.

"That's spicy," she managed to utter, but it was too late.

He told her that the food in Vietnam was disgusting; that the only thing he ate there was rice. The financial times back then were bad. Things have changed.

She felt bad for bringing him there. She did not consider indigestion or reflux.

"Will you let me sleep tonight?" He asked inside the Korean restaurant.

"Yes," she said, amused at his question. He probably remembered that on their first date she did not want to sleep.

As they left, she pointed to the Korean letters outside, spelling them out to him.

They rented movies later that day at Blockbuster Video. He would have preferred something else, knowing that all Blockbuster movies are censored. "Years ago, Blockbuster cut a deal with all the Hollywood producers. All movies rented at Blockbuster are to meet PG ratings. So, when you rent at Blockbuster, there are many scenes left on the cutting room floor." He also did not like Domino's Pizza. She guessed for the same reason why some people do not like Citgo—corruption. She wanted to get three movies from the discounted section: The Number 23, The Hoax, and Blades of Glory. She would have paid for them herself, but he paid. He told her to sign up for a card. When they got home, they watched The Pope of Greenwich Village and The Train, older movies. He fell asleep through part of the latter, with his feet resting on her coffee table. She combed his hair with her fingers, only wishing.

She woke him up so they could move to the bedroom. He fluffed his pillow and left traces of his scent.

The next morning, she got ready for work. He got ready for the plane. She cut out many things from her daily activities, so she'd have a few more minutes with him.

She took him to the couch and straddled him in his drawstring pants that he wore to the airport, kissing his face, his ears, his lips, his hair. His stubble gave her somewhat of a rug burn, but she did not mind. He kept telling her they should go, but she, keeper of the time, told him things will be okay. Right before they got up, he rested his head back while she continued to kiss him. He appeared satisfied for the moment.

* * *

After he returned home, she wrote him a poem:

"Stetson"
Every afternoon
around 5:30 or 6PM,
I arrive home
after a long day of work
to be greeted by
your scent.
Each morning
when I wake up,
I pick up the pillow
from the side where you slept
and take in a deep breath
through my nose.
Your scent fades
over time,
like my pain,
which is replaced with
more acceptance than I could have had
in the midst of it.
When the scent is gone
I will buy your cologne,
though I will never
be able to find the perfect blend
without your natural oils,
and I will spray that pillow
lightly
so that I have enough of you
to last me for years.

"Sweetness," he typed back in large font, always using large font to express intense joy. After he returned home, it was easier to ask him serious questions. To wait for face-to-face until their next outing would take too long.

"You, my dear, are an absolute delight," she said after their second date.

"And you are a queen!" he told her nobly, repeating what he said when he first pulled up to her apartment complex, with her dressed professionally in a business suit. (Yes, they saw each other on a weekday. She took one day of annual leave.)

"Then that would make you a king."

"Kind of. . ." he said, "Miss you and our magic."

It is around this time when they fantasized about living together in an exotic locale. Only after their second date. She mentioned the Asians in Mexico. He said that she could be a Korean person in Mexico who speaks Spanish. "I never said anything about being Spanish...hmm, I wonder what you are thinking," she said.

"Just carrying fantasy to different levels," he said with a devil icon, "Maybe learning Spanish is not a bad idea." He described to her his dream house, like the one he showed her on their first date, but with a surrounding veranda "in the foothills of somewhere cool." What a funny thing that he always told her he likes hot temperatures.

The next day she called him, but he had company over. Afterward he emailed her, "Hmm, you sounded rather lusty last night...I wish I did not have company."

A few days later, she got a call from the coworker who had her old car. He was a friend of Yue's. He asked her many questions, how she was doing, and so forth. She thought he already knew Yue and she were together. He did not. He just knew that they were emailing each other. Well, he found out then. He told her not to tell her boyfriend how long he had talked to her on the phone, lest her boyfriend be jealous. Her boyfriend was not the type to be jealous.

*　*　*

Ring!

"Hi. How are you?" Zarah answered.

"I'm surviving."

"What would you like to talk about?"

"I've been doing a lot of thinking lately about how short life really is. My roommate just overdosed the other day."

"Wow! Gosh, I'm sorry."

"I found a job. I even think I'll get promoted soon." She was glad to hear that he could stand on his own two feet without her. She thought he intentionally did not look for a job in order to hurt her. Sometimes she secretly wished that he would go to jail, not because she wished him harm, but because she did not. She felt that if he went back to jail that he would not need a job, would be fed/clothed/sheltered, and she would be able to safely communicate with him via letters and on the phone.

"That's good. What else is new in your life?"

"Well, some girl I had sex with told me that she was pregnant with my child, but it was all a lie so that she could get back with her ex. Why would someone lie about that?" Um…interesting share.

"Wow! That's crazy. I don't know why."

"I miss you. Why don't we stop playing games and get back together?"

"Uh…"

"We know each other so well. We've been together for over four years. We've been through hard times together. We lived together. No one will ever know you the way I know you." Through his calm, caring approach, she saw him as a sympathetic character, one who she would always care for, though she wasn't certain how. Then he added, "By the way, do you mind paying for a college class?"

"What do you want to take? How much is it?"

His answers were evasive and did not answer much. When she found out how expensive it was, she had to politely decline.

"Tying Loose Ends"
For someone who was given
the gift of life,
who am I
to give the gift of death?
'Tis better not to sin,
I say,
Better not to be a birth parent,
Better not to pass down

family curses, I say,
Better to know what I can
and cannot change.
It gives me power
and resolve
to do all I can do,
to sacrifice what I can sacrifice
(and still have enough to be fruitful),
to feel at peace,
to not be burdened
by fears, guilt, doubt,
to make an irreversible decision
in your favor,
in my favor too.
This is what God wants.
He has been telling me so
all along.
There is no turning back,
but there is a chance
that I will return.
The future cannot be predicted.
Anything can happen between
A and B;
I can create a path
leading back to you.

She thought about her answer for a little bit.
"You don't know me," she finally said honestly.

* * *

Unbeknowst to Yue, Threat had contacted her and finagled her into allowing him back into her life, if only for a brief moment, as he was able to arrange a plane trip out to Maryland.

Threat was so anxious to have sex that he wouldn't stop having sex with her even when she told him it hurt. She kept her eyes open the entire time. That experience cost her two weeks where it was too painful for her to go to the bathroom.

* * *

She complained via email that she was always forgetting her sunglasses. This is after her mom got cataract surgery in both eyes, and she was aware of the damage she was doing to her eyes. In response, Yue said, in a way that melted her heart, "You look great in dark glasses. You look great anytime."

Paranoid about her eyes again, she wrote to him: "I'm getting stressed out about my eyes. I passed by the bathroom mirror today and saw a bright red capillary. Did you notice that earlier this week? All I do is stare at a computer screen all day. Today, after I rubbed my eyes it took too long for my eyes to go back in focus."

"I love your eyes. . ."

"You always know what to say."

The next week she had too much pain in her eye. She tried to sleep on the bus so that it would be better when she got to work. When she got to work and could not open her eyes, she called for help. It was the security officer from the bus.

"How did you get here from Indiana?"

"Work," he shrugged.

Concerned about her, he drove her to the nearest Emergency Room and stayed in the waiting area with her since she did not own a car. The last time she was in the Emergency Room was when she was in Indiana. She remembered how much pain it was for the doctor there to sew up her self-inflicted wounds without anesthetic. That alone was enough pain to make her alter her habits. When the doctor called her in, he dyed her eyes so he could see them better and diagnosed it as a cut cornea. When he left to take care of another patient, the Indian man came in, and he told her that he felt guilty about what they had done, but that they were just having a little bit of fun. He loved his wife dearly and was more comfortable with her. He did not want drama, and he did not want her to have drama. He told her to take a chance on her boyfriend, get married, and have a good life. When the doctor returned, he gave her a prescription for an eye gel, and told her to sleep or stay in bed with her eyes closed.

CHAPTER 20

Birthday

"I miss you!" He told her twice in separate emails, not responding to what she sent, but uttering a cry that came from the pit of his stomach that he had to say it twice. In a few days, it would be his 65th birthday.

They reminisced about the first time they laid eyes on each other, or shall one say the third time. "I think I was undressing you," he told her sexily.

"I wish you could come and sit on my lap!' He continued.

"I want you," she told him.

"Likewise!!!!" He agreed with enthusiasm.

"So, are you brushing up on your Spanish?"

"One has to really immerse oneself!"

She suggested Rosetta Stone.

"I've seen Rosetta at the airports," he said.

She told him that she had considered being in the Air Force, like he was.

"Now that would have been very interesting and taken you to various locales."

"That's true. After having moved to one state, I want to try them all out."

"You could still do it!"

"I have always been a dabbler; it was my favorite Girl Scout patch."

"I'd love to see you in your uniform, sans underwear."

When she thought his birthday was coming around, she sent him a free e-Card and called him, but he did not answer. The next day the confusion was sorted out; she got the day wrong, even after that discussion they had earlier about his birth date.

His real birthday came around, and she sent pictures of her naked, covered only with Girl Scout sashes and vests. He enjoyed them, noticing the progression of age indicated by sash colors; they were like passports.

CHAPTER 21

Getting Serious (A Transformation)

She knew her future husband, and she knew her second husband. She was cheating on one of them with the other, but she did not know with whom she was cheating. When she held one, she held the other; when she thought of one, she thought of the other. When she saw one, she cried for the other; when she thought about leaving one, she remembered why it was so hard to do so. She wanted one with all her heart and needed one with all her head. She was the great caretaker lover. She felt needed; Yue needed someone younger, and Threat needed someone richer. Sometimes it is not true that there is someone for everyone. Sometimes there are two for one and none for another. She had two and Perez had none. The right combination of her two lovers would have made the perfect man, but life is not perfect, and we do not always get what we want. So, she held them both in her heart until she could decide who she was cheating on.

She would have waited decades if there were a promise that she would be reunited with one of them at the end of that wait. She would have bent over backwards and touched her toes. She would have left her family, her job, her friends, everything, if that was what it took to be with them. But which one deserved it?

She realized finally that many cheaters are not cheating because they do not understand the word "commitment," but rather that they got bored by seeing the same face every day in bed, or they didn't value what they had. She realized that many cheaters are just battling with the injustice of finding "the One" at the wrong time.

"All I Remember"
When I think of you
I see a black and white figure,
sometimes a silhouette.
Your face is blurry,
hazy, faded.
Sorry to say, but you
do not really turn me on
the way you used to.
I have stopped touching myself.
Perhaps I remember your laugh
most clearly
and your smell,
but that too will fade
until I hear and smell it again.
All that is left of you
in my head
is the memory
of loving you
because it is not a memory.
It remains close
like the back of my hand.

She chose to stay with the one who did not do her damage and the one she conversed with the most. Even though she held Perez in her heart, she was allergic to him. As with the (horrible) movie Hancock, they could not be together and stay alive, unscathed and unhurt. They had to scab their wounds by temporarily disengaging. If she told him she loved him, then there would be a financial consequence. There is an unspoken rule with them that she who has most must give to he who has least. So, she told Yue she loved him instead despite her love being as equal for them as for both sets of her parents. She was by nature a cheater; she could neither love just one man nor just one set of parents. She would often ponder Jesus's first commandment as she knew that within every blessing was a curse and within every curse a blessing.

She fooled people. She fooled her ex into thinking he had a chance by making the impossible sound possible, and she fooled her friends and family by making the possible sound impossible. She left a window of opportunity open for him. It was as large as the eye of a needle and required giving up one for the other. They were still desperate for that elusive thing that they could not give one another.

This is what she wrote to Perez, who wanted her with all his heart, soul, and mind:

"Babe,

We are still too close to the past, despite time and distance. For as long as we were together, it will take a longer time to heal; staying in touch with me will not help you to heal. To say I don't think about you would be wrong. I have forgiven you your wrongs, and I hope you forgive me, but that in no way means that getting back together will fix things. It hurts that you're hurting, but I would rather not hear the details along the grieving process until it's over; the only person you have right now is yourself. So, be your best friend and not your enemy. Learn, grow, and heal.

Your idea of love is staying together through thick and thin. My idea of love is that love makes people better people. I have not entirely given up on you yet, but these are the conditions I will need before we can move forward and not back:

1. When you can afford to buy a car and a plane ticket, then you will have paid your debt and may contact me so we can arrange an appropriate time for you to visit.

2. When you can convince my family and close friends who know about our past that we should get back together, then I may reconsider getting back together because I feel that it was my lack of a support

system that contributed to the past situation. If you can convince some, but not all, then I may at least let you stay in contact.

Until then, you are an ex. And you, more than anyone, should know the rules about exes who want to be more than friends.

Things will work out the way they are supposed to work out, and everything happens for a reason even if it's not what you want. Trust in God and believe in miracles. He always gives us what we need."

* * *

Ring! Ring! Ring! Ring! Ring! Ring!

If one were to create a painting that depicted this moment, it would look like a hand reaching out, stretched. The fingers would be made of sand and would be pulled by gravity downwards until there were no fingers left and no way to reach or to grasp.

As she sent her last communication to him, his shadow's stinger metamorphosed into claws. His old self was dead and gone.

* * *

"Sorting Opinions"
Something major,
something unusual has occurred.
The end is ambiguous,
the next step unclear.
I self-destructively seek
advice from friends
and strangers,
those who have been where I am
and those who have not.
After a while,
the conflicting advice
becomes a large inbox—stacked.
I get to the point,

like a woman,
where I wish to close off
my ears.
I wish to say that
I am the president
of my will,
in either sense of the word,
for deadlines do occur.
The decision rests here with me.
Some advice has been given
on the assumption that I am weak.
They do not know my resoluteness
nor my love.
Some advice has been given
from a lover's perspective.
I like it;
however, there is life to contend with.
The odds are against me.
Can I do it?
Can I earn nine gold medals
in money, career, emotions, distance, transportation, marriage, fertility,
health, and expectations—
one for everything I have the power to change?

As she expressed to Yue her own doubts about all their obstacles (finances, distance, age, family), he comforted her over the phone and told her, "It's fate, baby. Everything will be alright." She never forgot because she had a sense that she had cheated fate too, along with everyone else.

* * *

Ring! Ring!

The phone rang. She picked it up. "Hi wonderful," she said. She heard Yue blush thousands of miles away, surprised to hear that word.

* * *

"We need to talk about monogamy," she said, always needing to talk about the relationship like a woman who is too much woman.
"Yeah..." he said as he always does when he is ready to listen to her.

She told him her history. She told him about how many of her relationships had been non-monogamous and that when she was monogamous it was hard because she was used to the other way.
"The only boundaries are the ones you make for yourself. I would never be so presumptuous as to tell you what you can or cannot do," he said.

He told her his experience with swingers and threesomes and that it was not his thing.

* * *

Her boyfriend eventually wanted her to be non-monogamous, saying that she should find someone closer to her age, she had a failed first date with some other man who had gotten back from Vietnam but was not Vietnamese. There were no sparks. She had no feelings for him. It was awkward.

She came and told her boyfriend, "When I said that I was in deeper sooner than I'd expected, you said that I needed to date other guys because it wasn't fair to me. Well, I hope you do not mind me saying, but there are other men in my life who are very into me. However, they do not hold a candle to you. Their kisses are not good enough, they do not smell quite as nice, they are better for one-night stands or friends with benefits, they just do not compare to you. You are ichiban (#1)."
"I understand ichiban! My feelings are too, much more than expected. . ." he replied. Such words gave her hope, lasting hope.

They talked on the phone too about the issue:

"It sounds to me like you want us to be monogamous, right?" He asked.

She did not say anything but nodded at the phone. Due to this, she had to clarify, later, that they were indeed monogamous.

She told her close friend that she was monogamous with her boyfriend. Her friend found her amusing, "When the man you are with does not want you to be, then you are, and when you find a man who finally accepts your desire for nonmonogamy, then you want to be monogamous." She did find out later that Yue's great appeal to her at times had to do with his unconscious knack with reverse psychology.

*　*　*

"If you broke up with me now, I don't think I would know what to do. I need you right now. You are my therapy," she told him, as he knew that she need therapy from all that she had been through in the past. "No matter how much you feel about me I feel twice as much for you," she continued.
"Every time you go to sleep, take comfort in knowing that I think about you all the time," he consoled her.

*　*　*

Sometimes she would tell him about when she would get in arguments and disputes with her parents. He warned her with his insight, "Sounds like a rough day! Rule 1. Do not argue with your benefactors. Let me repeat... Do not argue with those who hold the purse strings (your parents). It gets you nowhere. Tomorrow will be a nicer day!"

*　*　*

"I am going to try to stop smoking," Yue said, "I need to take up some sort of activity to replace it, something like exercise, something like Tai Chi."
"Good."

Later...

"How's it going with trying to quit?" Zarah asked.
"It's very hard. I am not mentally prepared. It's like losing an old friend. How are your nails?"
"I am not mentally prepared."

*   *   *

Losing a friend is hard.
So, guess who called? Perhaps, they could just be friends. She didn't mention this to a soul.

*   *   *

Knowing that a certain newlywed was returning to work, she pulled him aside, not afraid that he was a complete stranger to her, and she asked if they could eat lunch.

At lunch, she asked him for the meaning of love and how did he know that he was in love.

(She asked the same questions in her letter to her birthmother, which she had translated by the adoption agency. Here reply was, "Marry the one who loves you, not the one whom you love.")

He spoke much of God in those answers to her. He told her, lucky guy, that he and his wife never had arguments that lasted more than half an hour. He told her that a woman wants to be loved, and a man wants to be respected. He told her that he grows more in love with his wife every day.

In her cubicle, he handed her a business card from his marriage counselor. She called the pastor up, despite the fact that she already had a counselor (thus she was cheating on her counselor too). She asked him, "How do I know if I am in love?" The first question he asked her was, "Would you be willing to let him go if you believed it was the best thing?" She could not then. He gave her 1 Corinthians to help her decide if she was in love. She talked to him on the phone. She would call him when she needed someone to talk to, but he was not as much help as her friends. He told her that for such a high-risk relationship that she should seriously sit down with her boyfriend, or talk to him on the phone, and put all the cards on the table. The earlier the better, for a high-risk relationship.

"We need to talk about the relationship and our expectations," she said to Yue, "I need to make sure that we are on the same page."
"Okay. Money is an issue. If I had more money, I would take you to some exotic place. If I had more money, I would take you to several exotic places around the world until we found a place to settle."
"Will you freeze your sperm for me?"
"Sure. That's your decision with what to do with it."
"And marriage?"
"If we get more serious, then that would be the logical next step."
"Will we live together in Mexico or live apart?"
"Oh, of course we'd live together. It doesn't make sense for us to live apart."
"My dad..."
"If the time were right, and we were really serious about each other, then I'd definitely sit down with your parents. I am sure that I can win them over. I can read people pretty well."
"Do you think your daughters will be okay with us?"
"They'll be fine. They already know I'm a little weird."
"Would you be okay with abstaining?"
"Sure, there will come a time when I won't be able to have sex."
"It may be a good idea to put together an extensive pros and cons list for if we stay together, and if we go separate ways. We could work on this together or apart. You can share or not; it's your choice."
"Ahaaa... The list maker..."

She never read her pros and cons list to him. She never told him that all the things she could do if they were apart were things she would still be able to do after he died.

After a pause, he said, "I think you are full of piss and vinegar."

"What?" she asked astonished, not having a clue what he just said. "It means you're curious."

* * *

Sometimes she would imagine the future. She would imagine that he would want to add her to his will, and she would tell him, "No, no. Save that money for your daughters." She would give them money too. She loved them without having met them, the way a birth family loves each other.

* * *

"We should talk about finances," she suggested the first night of August, "Tell me about your retirement account."

"I have no retirement account. None. Just Social Security. That's why I harp at you to begin a plan to stay on track and make and save money... The last couple of years I have saved some. It is still nowhere near six figures. That's why I have to look south to live."

It was from that conversation that the future looked, if not bleak, just very hard. They did not have much money.

Money was at a premium Yue reminded her, "And we should talk about these phone bills." She got the hint.

"I want you to establish yourself," he said, "That could take several years."
"It will take several years to be able to afford to live together. How about if I move back to Indiana? It would save me money on rent since the rent there is half what I am paying here. We should live together in the states before making a huge decision to move to another country."
"Absolutely not. You need to establish yourself."

Later that day she started freaking out, calling him up sequentially. When he answered the phone, she blurted out, "Will you wait for me? I feel selfish. Lie if you have to."
"Yes, if I were to lie to you, but really, we do not know what the future holds. I have never promised anything to you."
"No, you didn't."
"Have you been crying?"

Silence.

"Maybe," she said.

* * *

She sent him a pair of underwear, the sexiest piece she could find that she would not miss in her day-to-day life. She put it in an envelope. And he received it with great surprise and excitement. "Just got the mail... and your gift. I put them right to my nose and mouth to see if I could smell and taste you..."

* * *

A high school reunion was coming up for him in mid-August. He intimated that he wanted to go to show off. The popular people have been beset by the vestiges of age, and he still had his good looks, he said, though not in those particular words. She worried about him. Too much pride. It did not line up with 1 Corinthians. Eventually, he did not go, and she was glad. It would not look good to God. She asked him about his youth. He told her, "Back then there were the letter jackets, the brown jackets, and the Black jackets. I was a brown jacket."
"I have wanted to be so many things when I was young," she said, "a ballet dancer, a veterinarian, a director...What did you want to be?"
He responded, "I didn't think about that. I hated home. Like you, I have had a strained relationship with my parents. I could not wait to get out of the house. Having a car gave me my independence. That's what I cared about."

"I was not a studious student," he continued, "Ever since I can remember, as far back as grade school, I had extreme difficulty in memorization. Never could master the art of parroting back rote information."

"I'm the opposite. I am one of the rare breeds that actually liked school to some extent. I know, that's weird."

"It's not weird!"

"Did you have any extracurricular activities?"

"No. I hated sports. I was tall and lanky. Sports were awkward."

"I had a bad experience with physical education too. I was bullied a lot. Don't you hate it when people would hog the ball, so that you could never get a chance at it?"

"Yeah."

*　*　*

For the first time since their first date, he truly confided to her. He opened up a little more. He told her he was so frustrated at work and had no one else to vent to. He told her how he has difficulty saying "No," which makes his workload pile up. He told her about how people have taken advantage of his kind and giving nature, how a woman called him out of the blue who he had not seen for ages and asked him to call her boyfriend to make him jealous. He was able to find the word "No" for that situation. "One time a woman I have not seen for a while says she needs to stay somewhere for a night; she ends up staying for months. When she left, I was so relieved because that meant she was doing okay." As they get on tangents, he told her that he is not sure about his daughter's sexual orientation. They spent a longer time talking together. She always knew when she was reaching him when they talked longer times on the phone.

*　*　*

On the weekends he would work, being loaded down from all sides due to people taking their vacation at the same time. He was the jack-of-all-trades. He did shipping, receiving, parts, government sales, driving, whatever they wanted him to do he did. She would call him at work for a very few minutes because she knew it was no fun to work on the weekends. She also called for selfish reasons: just to hear his voice.

* * *

"Would you ever like to visit Korea with me?"

"Korea, sure. When one of us gets rich," he said, but he doubted that they would be able to afford it.

"I'm sure I could find something cheaper when I'm ready."

"Nothing is cheap anymore..." he said, "The world is fast changing. More than I have ever seen it in my life..."

"Yes, but I have hook-ups, connections to the Korean adoptee community," she said, not knowing if that would be enough.

* * *

"What I said on our first date, I have not taken that back. I love you," she told him over the phone.

"What you feel for me is lust," he said, not willing to believe in her.

"I do not," she said defiantly.

"Though I'm flattered, you are hanging your coat on me," he said, boiling their relationship down to a rebound, "I am just someone who showed you there are better fish in the sea."

"I have had other boyfriends besides you who treated me better than my ex."

"You 'love' me because I am unattainable."

"But you are attainable." She thought, <u>you</u> are the one that seeks the unattainable, sir. You act like a martyr, the way I did when I did not want to be happy, could not imagine being happy. You push away what you want. Why, sir? Because you are divorced?

The next day she talked to him via email and the phone about the possibility of having no sex when they saw each other next, partly to prove it is not lust, and partly because she wanted to know for sure that it was not.

"Projection"
My ex called me crazy
and wasn't I happy
when I learned that I wasn't!
I didn't have a problem
everyone told me. I am one of the most sane,
they said. You are strong, they said.
Then my boyfriend
did not believe my love.
This is a rebound,
he believed.
People try to connect dots
that do not exist.
I know what went wrong
with my ex.
I know what is wrong now.
These are two different matters
completely.
People imply that I am
crazy, but I can run circles around them
with my professional poise.
It never takes too long to find a better job.
People see "crazy" because I go all the way,
because I have Olympian faith,
because I have the Holy Spirit.
People project themselves on me,
they project their past and the fears they have
or had; they are jealous of my faith.
My boyfriend projects his own feelings
on me, claiming they are my own;
he is a pessimist.
No one around me,
even those who used to awe me
with their pious ways,
are quite as Christian, I feel.
I know what I do is right.
My childhood dream was always to go to heaven.

I look to my feet;
I am already many steps ahead. Faith
comes naturally.
My love is a God issue.
Take it up with Him.

CHAPTER 22

August

All seemed to be smoothed over by the next month. They continued their conversations.

When he told her, "One thing you should know about me, and that is, I am a news Freak!" she told him "I am just a [sex] freak."
"Albeit a beautiful freak!"

* * *

On the phone he said, "You should get basic cable."
"I don't want to. I am sick of TV. All my ex ever did was sit in front of the TV. I do not ever want to see another TV again."
"But you are out of the loop."
"I'll think about it."
"Get basic cable. Some cable outfits also offer basic cable plus (a few more channels), for a few bucks more. Again, they will not tell you about the service, you have to press them on this. Cable companies are licensed to serve the community they are in. If they do not respond in an appropriate manner, then you can go to the licensing authority."
He added, "It should not cost more than $15 a month."
"But every penny counts, to me," she replied.

Of course, with enough persuasion and persistence from his end, she got it... temporarily.

*   *   *

When she had another mystical revelation, he told her, "In the last 17-20 years, I have learned a lot. Every day is a step forward. You are starting to get it. Makes my heart go." Just reading that made her heart go too.

*   *   *

Out of curiosity, she asked about the woman who replaced her on the job. Teasingly, she asked him if he had been flirting with her. He told her that she was the only one he had been flirting with.

*   *   *

Talking of replacements...

Her personalized ringtone for Perez sounded.
"I have a girlfriend."
"What's she like?"
"She's a lot like you; she likes to write poetry."
"Does she know your secrets?"
"Yes."
"Wow! I'm surprised. It took you months and years to tell me your secrets."
"She subscribes to a newsletter for people who monitor the courts."
"How does she feel about exes?"
"She thinks it's cool that we can still be friends."

*   *   *

A few days later...

"I'd like to sing to you..." she said, knowing what to sing.
"I like the song you sing when I am eating you," he confided.

Later, she sang to him "You're the One That I Want" from Grease, the musical.

"I could just kiss you," he said, tickled at her.

"I can do better than I did. I just get a little nervous when I am singing to someone."

"You were wonderful!"

* * *

They talked about Pink Floyd. He said that was old music, old to him. It was new to her.

* * *

Then there was the key scenario. She thought she had lost her keys, but someone found them dangling from her front door and turned them into the leasing office.

"You will not believe the bad luck I have had today. Somehow, I lost my keys. I had them yesterday. Now, who knows? I got a copy made at Home Depot from my mom's copy, but the outside key does not work very well, being that it is a copy of a copy, which I also secretly think is a copy of a master key. Unfortunately, the key to my safe is gone too. All the stuff inside it is safe, including a particular stash, but I cannot get to it. It has been a bad luck day."

"Pray to St Anthony. He is the patron saint of lost items. No kidding."

"I was doing some physical labor today to get my mind off the losing of the keys. My mom had wanted me to put together some shelf/table thing for Dad's birthday. So, looking through the instructions, which I could have done far better, I figured it out. I bet you would have liked to watch me bend myself in weird positions on the floor as I was trying to figure it out."

"I would indeed!"

"Been going through a lot of emotions lately due to the loss of my keys. It makes me feel helpless, hopeless, angry. I really wish I had more money. I wish I could afford more independence."

"Yup."

"Maybe you've picked up on this, but I have always hated reality. I cannot stand to live in it; it gets to be unbearable. From a young age, I have sought escapist venues. I am a writer because I was good at English, and I was good at English because I wanted to escape through books. And then I found romance. Well, but even when I think I have found the solution to leaving reality in the dust, it still creeps up on me. I am a little depressed. Life has not been what I wanted it to be."
"Life never is. Suck it up."

Later...
"Oh, thank God!! The prayers to St. Francis worked. I called the apartment office and someone turned them in. I had, as I suspected, left them in the door. That sure put me in a tizzy. So, as I always believe, things happen for a reason, and that reason is that now I have a copy made for you. Yes, I trust you that much. This will be good for times when you arrive before I am off work or if you are here when I am at work and want to do stuff outside."
"St. Francis must have turned your request over to St Anthony. He is the patron saint of lost stuff."
"Hehe, yeah. Got confused."
"Do you think those guys use e-mail?"

When she found her original keys, she lost the copy she had just made for Yue. She had nothing to mail him. When they turned up, the keys were lost in transit.

* * *

Another time they talked about the movie Elegy, based on the book The Dying Animal by Philip Roth. The actors in it were Ben Kingsley and Penelope Cruz. The age-gap was similar to theirs. Yue told her that he heard about it from the TV. She read about it in the newspaper. She would like to see it one of these days. They finally did end up watching it later.

* * *

They flirted constantly. "My [computer] mouse has become harder to move," she complained.

"I have a big mouse for you" he said, wide grinned she bet.

"If I were there, I would sneak up on you and plant a big kiss on you when you least expected it. The very thought of you makes me purr..."

"And you awaken my ___!"

"Meow."

"Stoke my fire. You make my naughty parts tingle."

She told him that she was well known for speed and efficiency at work.

"I love to slow you down," he said in reply.

"Staying still is not fun when it's cold," she would say. The cold was something to which they could both relate.

"The cold turns on your headlights."

"There are several people who have my name," Zarah said, despite it being rare.

"None as beautiful as you."

"I can't stop thinking about making sweet love to you."

"Same. I can't wait to make out with you."

"I would like to make love to you every single day."

"Agreed."

"I've gone into the restroom a few times when I think about you during the day (if you catch my drift)."

"I do! You will have to tell me about it sometime."

"You make me so horny that I just have to disappear into a fantasy world for a while."

"Only a few more weeks!"

"I want you to lick my neck and put your fingers through my hair."

"More...agreed."

"I want to suck you all night long."

"I would not last. Would have to enter you."

"I will be tame while we are both at work, but underneath are layers of passion."

"Tame in name only."

"Virtual kisses."

"And to you!"

"Just got the mail. Kisses to you..." (The mail contained a poem about faith and belief.)

"I love to make memories with you," Zarah said.
"We will too!"
"Wish you could smell my fingers."
"Been in the ladies' room again, eh?"
"Would you like it if I dressed up like a schoolgirl for you?"
"Sure...sans panties."
"I have a world to offer you."

Her favorite flirtation was when he told her, "You are the most beautiful in all of the countries."

CHAPTER 23

Mid-August Fun

When she wanted to talk about relationships, he seemed to be in the mood for sex. She froze a little in her mind. It took her a while to realize it was partially her fault...all those lustful emails were to blame.

He came to town again on work. He doubted that they would have the time to see each other due to the short amount of time he would be there. Knowing how much she regretted seeing him the first time he was in town on business, she called him up and spent money toward cab fare. The taxi driver said that he was just there and now has been asked to go there again.

When she saw Yue, he waited for her outside, excited to see her. When they made love, they did it to "Falling Into You" by Celine Dion, a woman he says is too "white bread" and mainstream, but the song was good. Ironically, Dion's husband was around Yue's age and had a seven-year old child.

"Put your hands on the wall," he told her as she was on top. That was better. Afterwards he poured them some chardonnay, leaving an unopened bottle for her to bring back to her apartment.

In the morning, they rushed to get ready and rushed out to the red truck. She did not have much space to sit, but she was skinny, at least then. They left the parking lot as she helped him to see parts of the road that he could not see.

"You cannot get pregnant," he told her in the car at a stoplight, squeezing her hand sternly, and "If you do, you must get an abortion. Understand?"

"Yes," she said, not feeling very happy.

As he was waiting to drop off the truck at the port, they made love like exhibitionists, while not exhibiting anything to anyone. They kissed a lot. She let herself go weak in his arms, and he moved her body from side to side. She leaned her bottom half toward him. They hid up against a large truck door, and she briefly sucked him, with her head against the floor of the vehicle, until he moaned aloud. She pulled back so that they would not be caught, but that instant of pure pleasure in a few seconds could thrill her for a lifetime. Despite their passion, she saw herself from the outside.

"I love your pictures. How did you learn to model like that?"
"It comes naturally."

They walked elsewhere, with his sealed-lip coworker, to wait for a taxi.
"Let's go inside," Yue said.
"I thought you liked the heat."

He, thinking that she was a computer geek ("You are so geeky!" he would tell her) even though she was just a product of the Information Age, asked her if she knew how to do this or that. She could not help him.

They went to the airport next. They sat in the back seat while they took a brief nap with each other.

They found a place at the airport where they could eat since she did not have a plane ticket and could not go through the metal detectors because of it. They ordered. She got fish and chips. It took a while to get their order, but not too long. He turned her hand over, looking at the palm of her hand and caressing it with his finger, memorizing it. He talked to her over a badly made Philly cheese steak, but she did not hear what he said. "What do you think?" he said next.

"I think you're sexy," she told him to make him blush. "May I see your driver's license?" she asked. He handed it to her. "Your driver's license says that the color of your eyes are blue," she said. "Your eyes," she continued, "change color. They are blue on the outside and greenish-brown on the inside. Are your eyes hazel by any chance?"
"You know, I never thought about it," Yue mused.

She was impressed that she was the only person to notice. What sort of lovers did he have before her?

"I do not like my hair. I want to dye it," Yue said.
"If you really wanted to dye your hair to look younger, I would not feel different about you one way or the other. However, I would like you to consider that I love the way you look now."
"I'll never get around to it..."

When he left to go through the metal detectors at the airport, he pulled her over to a glass column, giving her the most passionate, intense kisses she felt that she had ever known from him. She has melted several times afterwards, upon the thought of it happening repeatedly in her mind.

Before he left, he whispered to her, "When I think about you, I breathe a little faster."

"White-Haired Man"
White-haired man
I'm falling deeply in you.
White-haired man—
I know, I know,
I know how to take you.

White-haired man
Aha, Aha! The world is seeing
romance then
with me and you,
you white-haired man.

White-haired man,
I'll inject life back in you.
White-haired man
I'll be there when you have nothing,
nothing left.

Feel the rhythm of my body.
Feel the body of my breath.
Feel me captivate you.
I'll love you even when you have nothing,
nothing left.
Love you forever,
like the sun loves the sea.
Love you like
we are the only ones left
with life.
Feel the rhythm of her body.
Feel the body of my breath.
Aha Aha You see
You are the end of my path.

* * *

The next day she wrote to him, "When I think about you, I breathe a
little harder myself. You make my heart race."
"Have already been thinking about our next date!'"
"Have been breathing a little harder...You know what I mean."
"My thoughts sometimes trail to where yours are."
"You make my heart beat faster, and you leave me breathless."
"Breathless...ahh."

However, she still felt a little numb with discomfort after thinking about their last meeting too much and vented via email about how she felt used, like a body. He was not so crass, he told her. Instead of being upset at her for making accusations he said, "You are a remarkable woman." Perhaps it was because of the way she said something. She did not remember.

She apologized, "As you can tell, my mood changes fairly easily. God, I wish I were not so female!"
"Am sure glad you are!!!!"

She called him, expecting him to be somewhat upset, but he talked of other things and laughed a little, teasing her, when she brought up her rant. That is what she loved about him. It did not help, with someone as emotional as she was, to fuel the fire. That is what her ex did. Yue, on the other hand, was everything she wanted her ex to be. He always smothered her flames with mental kisses. Then her frustrations dissipated like smoke.

They talked tangentially on the phone until he was ready to hang up.

"Wait. I never got to say what I wanted to say," she said, realizing that she was being distracted, wondering if it was a technique.
"Sure, what is it?"
"I would never get pregnant on purpose, but I just don't like the way you forced me into saying 'Yes' by the way you asked the question about abortion. It was the way you said it."
"That's me being an ass."
"But I am going to do something that you do... If you were twenty years younger, I would love to have a son with you."
"Oh, for sure," he says. Fersher.
"Our prodigy would be interesting," he said, "what with your Korean features and my Scandinavian ones."
He just barely eked out faint words of hope, in a half-whisper, "If it were to happen, we would figure something out."

* * *

Later, he told her that he may go to the Renaissance Fair in his town after work.

"Man! I wish I could go with you!" she exclaimed.
"Me too!"
"If I were there...When there was no one around, I'd sit in your lap and wrap my legs around you, holding you and kissing you passionately with the office door closed."
"When I am there, I'd like some quiet time, where we just lay on the bed and explore each other... Taking our time."
She would tell him her dreams, of bumping into him at the local grocery store seeing him dressed up all in black.

"I bet you never thought about it, but you would look stunning in black slacks with a black shirt," she told him.
"I have and I do. Also, with black jeans, black/charcoal t-shirt, and a dark grayish sport coat and black baller shoes."
"Do you own anything leather?"
"Couple of leather jackets." Purr!

$$* \quad * \quad *$$

They fell back into their usual flirtations:

"You rev my engine," she started.
"The excitement begins to grow."
"In your pants."
"Big time."
"I bet you want some help with it."
"Love it when you hold it."
"Love it when I can taste it."
"Mmmmm."
"Many kisses everywhere."
"You are very frisky today."

"You were very frisky today," He repeats later in the day.
"I wish I were there to help lighten your [work] load."

"Put a load in you."
"I'm sooo ready for you to whisk me off to paradise."
"Your mind is wandering again."
"Kiss."
"It all starts with a kiss."
"It may rain Sunday."
"Love to make love during the rain."

Sometimes when they were not talking about sex, they would take the time to be silly, enjoying life. When she would rant about various, unrelated topics she would type, "The Attack of the Barrage of Emails."

* * *

"Good morning," she said.
"To wake up with you...what a treat!"

CHAPTER 24

A French Classic

The main topic of conversation with her counselor was true love. Every week she would ask Zarah, "What is love?" Every time Zarah replied, her counselor would ask if her definition applied to lovers as equally as to friends, family, and God. If they did not, then it was back to square one, back to the drawing board. She would pray to God that she would know the meaning of love. She would read relationship books that counseled her to love people unconditionally to prepare herself for loving God.

* * *

"Dear Zarah"
You claimed that you
loved him.
Many doubt your feelings,
but if you
affirmatively answer all
my questions
then I have no doubts
your love was true.
If he were not ready,
would you have waited,
even if he died first?

Would you have
waited decades
to be with him,
hoping he was still alive?
Would you continue
to love him
despite incompatibilities
and other handicaps?
Would you have
prayed for his health
every day until he died?
Would you have
continued to pray,
after his death,
that you could join him
one fine day?
Would you have called to him
as he lay in his grave
with a bouquet of flowers
and asked him
to wait for you
until bodily
distinctions mattered no more?
In your death,
are you holding his hand?

Even though she had already watched one film set in France with him, he recommended that she watch another, a French classic.

She did not want to give away the plot, but the movie was tragic, like Shakespeare's Romeo & Juliet.

Someone killed himself out of love for someone else—his niece, but he did not know that it was his niece. The woman absolutely detested him, despised him for a crime he committed, an unforgivable sin, and he could not live with her thinking such thoughts of him.

In real life, the actors got married and had a daughter only to get divorced.

As she watched, she saw the feelings for her own love grow, bloom, and reach its hand out of the cage of "not love." She felt her love grow believable, strong, and able to endure anything. She also felt her faith grow.

She watched this movie after her counselor had requested that she make a list of why she loved Yue. When she looked at her list, she noticed that her motivations were as pure as gold.

When he asked her how she liked the movie on the phone, she teased him, "You seem to have a thing for movies with unhappy endings. That will have to change." However, one cannot change people; they can only change themselves.

CHAPTER 25

Labor Day Weekend

She told Yue that there was a wine tasting event in town for when he would be over for their fourth date. He sounded interested. She thought back to his progression of age. He grew more stunning while he stayed single, on a shelf somewhere waiting for the right person to drink him up. Things were definitely going well between them. They decided not to go camping with her friends and thought that she might get to introduce him to them at a later point in October as her mystery man.

On his trip to the East Coast, he visited with his daughters before he visited with her. The youngest was ten years older than her. This was different from what she thought he would do when they talked about it in June: "When I come out on my own this summer," he said then, "I plan to spend a few days with you before I go into the city to see my daughter. If that works for you..." When he arrived at one of his daughters' place, he told her that his granddaughter was asleep.

"What is your granddaughter's name?" she asked via email.
He told her. Funny, she had always wanted to name a child that name.
"I can hardly wait until tomorrow!"
"Very exciting!"

The day of his arrival she woke up early and spent all day getting ready. She Swiffered the floors. She wiped down the counters, the sinks. She cleaned the toilet. She plucked her eyebrows and painted what nails she had left. She curled her hair and did not like the result, so she put her hair in ponytails and curled the hair in the tail ends. She tried to throw together a sexy schoolgirl outfit especially for him from the miscellaneous items that she had. She forgot where she put her knee-highs. She applied and re-applied makeup. Her eyeshadow color changed many times before he came, from blue to green then with the final color being a smoky black. She tried various colors on her lips and added gloss. However, she was most worried about the hideous pimple on her face. She applied and reapplied concealer.

"I will be there in ten minutes," he said as she was already preparing the place for his arrival, opening the shades, letting the light in. She greeted him with high-pitched excitement on the phone, letting him know that she was ready.

She gave him her parking pass and waited for him to walk through her back door. It did not take long for them. She put her left leg up so he could put his hand under her skirt and grab her thigh. They walked into the bedroom, and she wiggled her butt, with her hands on the back of her computer chair, beckoning to him to come get it.

"You look so beautiful with those earrings on," he said after they had changed positions, while he was on top of her, while she was gloriously naked.

During their sexual romp, she told him, "Wait a second" and got some chocolate syrup out of the fridge. Yum!

After they made love, she played some songs, some he did not like, and the ones he did were his own. However, she also played her song for him: "Head Over Feet" by Alanis Morrissette (she also liked to think of him with "What's It Gonna Be?" by En Vogue and "Like You'll Never See Me Again" by Alicia Keys). He liked that song by Alanis Morrissette. As he took a nap post-massive orgasm, she spoke to him in French so that he could not understand. She told him that he was wonderful, handsome, good, likeable, adorable, and magnificent, etc. He listened to the words he could not understand and told her to go to sleep.

When he was awake, he never commented on her apartment even though it looked very different from the last time he was there. He did not make any observations. He was not curious like she was the first time she had sex with him.

In the morning, they went to have breakfast with their newspaper in hand. He got the front page. She got everything else. She ordered a Belgian waffle.

"You see that girl over there?" He said, "I'm attracted to girls like that. She is maybe 5-10 pounds over, but that is okay. I like dark-haired beauties."

"But your daughters are blond. Your ex-wife was blond."

"Strawberry blonde. What kind of men are you attracted to?"

"Oh, I don't know. They are all very different. I guess I'm attracted to whoever looks like the person I'm dating."

He started to talk about her parents' sex life then, and she told him to stop.

"How tall are you? 5'6'?"

"Yes."

"5'4" would be too short for me, but 5'6" is the perfect height so that I can kiss you."

"I was reading a book about how women need love and men need respect. I don't feel that your wife respected you." She did, after all, get pregnant twice without alerting him or discussing children.

"There was not much to respect," he said.

"I respect you a lot for all that you have been through. When I think of you, I think of strength. I admire the strength and character you have developed over the years from tough situations (divorce, dysfunctional family, and the succeeding trials, etc.). I respect your desire to pay for my meals. I respect you and would never cheat on you because to you that is a respect issue." Okay, so, she never actually said all of that, but it was on the tip of her tongue.

She was reading that relationship book mostly to understand what went wrong with her ex. Her coworker's marriage counselor and pastor had recommended it to her. She proceeded to tell Yue about her findings, about the mnemonic devices used to help couples. She was hoping that they could have a sincere discussion about it, but he waved her away saying that all that is theory. They talked instead of things they would like to do for fun.
"I'm going to scan the pictures I have from when I was younger."
"Stop telling me about it and just do it," she said annoyed, "You've been telling me that for months."

He paid for their breakfast and they left.

As they rode in the white rental car, she asked him naively, "Did you tell your daughters anything?"
"There are just some things you do not say to your kids, and this is one of them."

She remembered how he told her that he thought his daughter liked girls and thought that if he could not tell her this, how could she tell him that? She had already told her mother that she was bisexual and that she was dating someone decades older than her. Suddenly, she remembered when he told her that they would have no problem with their relationship. Did he lie to her, or did something wake him up from his dreaming state?

He told her how much he loved being single.
"But you're not single. You're with me," she said, "but it seems like you are used to being single."
"Yes, I haven't lived with someone else for a long time."

After having known him to be a sweet, understanding, accepting man, she felt rejected by him from all angles that day. He did not like the music she played nor did he want to see the movies she liked. He did not know anything about her, nor did he seem to care. He just liked the memories she gave him to get him through old age, altering reality to be his fantasy despite how much he was initially afraid of fantasizing.

At a stoplight, she took a candid photo of him with her camera phone. He did not want her to take his picture, but it helped her get through the days. He would not deny her that.

When he had arrived yesterday, he was two hours behind schedule because his suitcase got lost. Then it was found. It was somewhat destroyed. He was using a brown leather belt to drag it.

They Mapquested Burlington Coat Factory. He looked at the selection and did not like what he found. He found the right brand (again with the Tommy Hilfiger; is that a default male brand?) in the wrong color. She pointed out the frivolous-looking girly suitcases. He said that she would look good with them. She did not feel very complimented even though she guessed she could see herself with them when she was a few years younger.

"These are baller shoes," he said as they passed by Men's Shoes because she did not know what they were.

He said something in Hebrew as they walked away from the Burlington Coat Factory in Burlington, Indiana to try to replace his suitcase that was damaged by the airlines. "I know some Jewish because I used to date a girl who was Jewish. We used to live together."
"I have been to a Bat Mitzvah once," she said.

They walked to Blockbuster to buy some movies to watch. When she pointed out some things she wanted him to watch, he, somewhat rudely, made it clear that he wanted to do things his way. She felt that he did not think he would like what she liked. They entered the grocery store to pick up a few minor supplies. They passed by a Vietnamese bar and walked inside, downing a few drinks while their groceries warmed to room temperature.

When they returned to the apartment, she ordered a pizza. He paid her back in cash. "You know there are over forty years between us. That's a lot," he began.

"Yes, two generations." Only one generation in her family.

"You know, I am going to have to break up with you one day. It is going to be hard," he said. Her heart dropped a little into her stomach. Even though he had said so before, she felt that it had come out of nowhere. She wished that she had had some warning.

"I may want to go to Korea or Vietnam or somewhere in the Africa francophonie someday. I will want to write to someone," she hinted.

"You can write to your journal," he said, not budging. But then he softened up. "That night you told me you like me, we both really wanted to kiss each other, didn't we?" He asked.

"Yes," she replied. Oh yes.

"I wanted to kiss you."

She went to his suitcase and put his well-worn jean shirt around her, tying the ends like it was a midriff top. It was, most likely, the shirt she saw him in the first day she met him.

"You're so sexy," he said to her with his work jacket over her silk blouse, tied under the middle of her bra.

They went out, and she introduced him to a patbingsoo, a Korean dessert. Later, he told her that it was so good that he could still taste it when they were in bed.

When they came home, he shaved because she had pointed out his stubble. Not wanting to, but doing so anyways, he warmed his face with a wet washcloth and covered his face in white lather. She watched each stroke of the razor against his clean face. Left cheek, right cheek. She watched him shave from his neck to his chin. She watched him become less stubbly. She watched as she wished to be a blade on his razor, just to be that close to him.

"It was a lazy day today," he said.

"Yes, it was," she smiled, knowing that it was a nice break from his work.

"I was thinking about emailing you some porn."

"Cool."

Tired from the long day, they sat on the couch watching a movie. He knew exactly what he liked in music and movies. "Am not familiar with current movies... Have not been in a movie theatre for over 15-20 years. We each reserve the right to veto. If I am in a movie theatre and the dialog becomes stupid, or the story becomes stupid, I leave. Sometimes I ask for my money back. I refuse to sit through stupid movies."

She popped the DVD into the DVD player. Only one movie they rented was decent enough to watch, but he gave it a "C, maybe a C+" rating. While they watched the movie, she would comb her fingers through his white hair from time to time.

* * *

"Second Attempt"
I am trying again
to understand the difference
between a woman and a man.
I am hoping that
counseling and certificates
and degrees and titles
will strengthen my understanding,
no, our understanding,
of how to communicate
love and respect.
I am remembering
what not to do.
Perhaps it will steer
our ship.
Perhaps anyone can be loved,
but it must be done right,

with sincerity,
with honest appreciation
that the other is alive.
I can give everything I have.
I can wait.
I can pray.
I can communicate.
You, failed first marriage.
Me, failed engagement,
twice.
You and me,
we have the power,
strength, and will
of God behind us.

That evening, she decided to approach a topic that had been plaguing her. She spoke to him while they lay in bed with his back turned to her and her arm around his stomach. His skin was smooth.

"In that movie you recommended I watch, I would not say that I would kill myself for you as one character did, but I certainly relate to the feeling," she said, probably not the smartest thing she has ever said in hindsight. "I would die for you," she continued.
"You will never have to."
"I would do anything for you."
"I know, but I would never exploit it."
"Well, you can."
"Well, I won't."
"I will never judge you; you do not judge me."
"That is true."
"You do not have to do anything for my love. I give it willingly. All you have to do is be yourself. I will continue to love you even when you do not love me. You can never understand my feelings."
"The more you tell me, the more I understand."
"It hurts me to be with you; it makes me sad because you keep saying it is temporary."
"At some point I will have to say it is the end, but I will not want to."

"Even after we part, I will still see you in the future." She did not say that she will want to see him, she said that she would see him. "God played a cruel joke on me," she cried out.

"God did not do anything to you."

"I will love you even if we were not compatible."

When he left for a minute to go to the bathroom, she asked him, "Do I talk too much?"

"Yes, but I understand why," he said, always understanding her.

He went back into bed with his back to her once again. His smooth skin rested against her breasts.

"I will love you forever," she told him in desperation, "You cannot say anything to change my mind."

"I'm TOO OLD!" he growled at her, almost like a desperate plea, a desperate whine, with his back turned to her in bed.

"That's not going to work," she said, bitter that he tried to bite through the chain of love that she had entangled him in. What a poor man he was to have met her!

She continued to tell him, in exasperation, how strong her love is for him until she heard snores coming up like smoke. She had spoken for too long. It had been a long day.

He got up again later in the night to use the bathroom.

After he returned from the bathroom break, she waited until it almost seemed like he was asleep and asked, "Are you awake?"

"Yes," he said, "How did you know?"

"If I ever go to Mexico or Panama, it will be for me, and we will live separately."

His understanding came in the form of silence.

In the morning, they made passionate love quickly so that she could get ready for work, and he could get ready for the plane ride to his home.

They quickly hopped into the shower as they cleaned each other with soap, most lovingly, as if her feelings for him did not scare him off even though she knew it did.

For many minutes, they made love by the screen door. He, not knowing the time, was anxious to leave, in worries that she would miss her bus to work. Outside in the parking lot they made love clothed, repeatedly, clinging to what they feared could be lost. Much of the kissing was broken up by strings of long-term hugs, the goodbye sort. He broke away, went to his car, and she went toward the direction of her bus.

"Wait!"

She turned around.

"Your parking pass..." He said as they melted back into each other's arms one last, final time.

He left before she remembered what she wanted to do when he was here. He never got to see certain creations she had made nor pictures that had been taken of her. Perhaps it was for the best. Such a thing would have reminded him of her youth.

Yue called her when he returned home. He told her with awe that they both have so much energy for each other, being apart for long stretches of time. She told him she was just thinking about that as she moaned into the receiver as she touched herself. He listened for a while, perhaps too tired to respond in kind.

She was glad to have had the opportunity to get her feelings out about how much she loved him. However, her relief was soon to become regret. They separated two days later.

CHAPTER 26

Separation

It was that time of year when people separated. Two of her coworkers, not related to each other, had separated from their spouses within practically the same day. They were pretty young too. One took time off from work.

Suddenly the mood between Zarah and Yue changed. She emailed him the following:

"I would like to say 'I understand you' as you have said to me before, but I will not profess to fully understand. I will never be where you are. However, I can try to put myself in your shoes. If I were in your position, my mind would be riddled with doubt and bad memories of times when I had or I had witnessed someone else having had large disappointments based on large dreams fading slowly or being quickly torn apart. I can tell that it is hard for you to open yourself to me.

There are two ways to react when faced with a difficult situation, both of which have already been expressed. There is your way of pulling back so that you minimize your own hurt and thereby increase mine (unrequited love is so painful). Then there is my way of believing and praying and never giving up. Choices...choices..."

He did not reply. She considered not writing him in anger to see if he would miss her or if he would never write back. She talked with a male coworker about it, without too much detail, and he agreed that maybe that was the right choice. Men, he agreed, were takers.

Never knowing that this time would come, she felt something in her heart that told her they should separate. With faith.

Knowing what she would do, she called her father, thankful to get rid of a deep secret, thankful to include him back in her life. She told him everything. He carefully figured out what to say, much of which she did not like. He told her that she had only herself to blame, that she could not trust her judgment, and that she needed to follow good advice. He said she was incapable of just having male friends. He told her that she had destructive behaviors, that there must be something wrong with her boyfriend, that she jumps from relationship to relationship, that she needed to find something she enjoyed that is not a human being...

"You have zero confidence and self-esteem. You have only yourself to blame. Look in the mirror and know who did this."
She thought, Am I to blame for falling in love?
"You should do volunteer work and give back to the community. If you want someone to love there is me and your mother, your aunt and uncle. Four people who are safe to love."
She still felt hesitant about such a thing, they were not the people she trusted the most in her life with her feelings. They were not there for her when she was in an abusive relationship.
"You intentionally complicate your life."
No, what she wanted more than anything in the world was for her life to not be complicated.
"You will need at least a year and a half to fix yourself," Dad says, "So what are you going to do?"
"I can find a second job," she said, having already thought about it.
"Why?"
"So that I can be independent and pay off my debt."
"That is all good, but you need to find a purpose. Read a Purpose-Driven Life."

She felt like she had so much room to grow. She patiently thanked him for the advice before he left her apartment, and he thanked her for her honesty.

She called Yue to tell him what she felt she must do. He answered as he had always done, with a sound in his voice that said he was happy to hear her. He concurred, relieved to have gotten a way out. After all, he told her that he would have to break up with her, not wanting to, of course. His attitude intimated that they still had time, but she knew herself and knew that she could not be in an unbalanced relationship at that point in her life. With great difficulty, she said those things that she felt about how they were at different points in our lives. "This is the most difficult thing I have ever had to do," she said between tears. At the sound of her tears, she heard a different voice in him, a soft, tender, controlled voice as he uttered sounds of listening, almost like a lamb. She could almost tell that he believed she loved him.

She needed to "find herself," meaning that she needed to feel comfortable being alone in her own skin. (How ironic it was that her childhood passion of self-improvement now brought with it the sadness of being apart from the one she loves!)

"I told my father because I knew what I had to do today."
"He must have been surprised!"
"Yeah. I cannot be in an unbalanced relationship. I think you're a bit of a commitment-phobe, being divorced and all."
"I'm not afraid of commitment."
"Well, okay…"
"And the age thing…"
"Age has never been an issue!" The only boundaries are the boundaries you make for yourself.
"Well, okay. So, how do you want to do this?" He asked. She told him, as before, that she would return, and that she would always love him.
"Do you believe in my word?" she asked him.
"I do not plan for the future," he said, dodging her.

"Don't go!" she yelled forth, the decibels changing, the fear getting thicker, "This is the last time I get to talk to you. Well, the last time for a very, very long time. How do you feel about me?"
"I am not where you are. We'll leave it at that."
"I will miss you so much."
"I'll miss you too."
"Will you stop thinking about me?"
"No."
"I will love you forever."
"Go to bed," he whispered.

After a few seconds, she called him up again.

"Sorry," Zarah began.
"Why?"
"For calling you again." He laughed.
"God, I'll miss your laughter so much."
She continued to the point she wanted to bring up, "Keep me up-to-date on your contact information."
"I will do that. Go to sleep."

After many prayers to God, prayers in which she had been asking to find true love, she finally found true love, and it continued to break her heart. She had also selfishly prayed, asking for Yue and her to be together. That prayer was not answered, at least not yet. Yue was easy to love. At his age, she accepted him exactly the way he was, continuing to do so. Now it was hard to love him, but it never ended. Now she only prayed for good health, not necessarily just her own.

CHAPTER 27

The Break-Up

Being that there were two men who held her heart, she decided to call up the other man with whom she might have a chance. She knew he was still with someone else, so that made her tailor what she said to him.

"Please listen to everything. I couldn't decide what to tell you, so I have five things to say. Choose one to focus on."

"One, part of the reason why I left you was because I felt disrespected. You seemed to think that I would always jump into your lap and that you didn't need to win me over. I'm not trying to point out flaws, but I want to say, 'Please respect her. Don't treat her the way you treated me.'

Two, if you marry and have kids, then I will not be able to return.

Three, I broke up with Yue…because he's not you."

"Of course."

"Four, I have poetry that I could send you about feelings I had about you, but I don't know if it would be wise to dredge up the past.

Five, it's nice that she thinks it's good that exes can still be friends, but what she knows is only a half truth. I don't think we should communicate while you're with someone else. It would be better for me and for her. And I probably should not have told you anything else I told you today."

"So, it's my fault."

Amelie was taken aback.

"OK, so you want to focus on the negative," she said, "Do you love me?"

"I used to."

"I love you, but that doesn't seem to matter much." She hung up. He had put her in the discard pile.

* * *

She called the only person she knew who could help her in this time. Of all the people she could call, she called the ex before her ex, not her parents. She called the man who rescued her from Threat. Someone who has known her a long time, someone whom she trusted with her emotions, someone who truly understood in every way what she was going to endure.

As they got high, she told the man who loved her about her love for another man, Yue, as he listened patiently, always understanding every word.

"You got your revenge," she told him bitterly, thinking of the song "What Goes Around" by Justin Timberlake.

"I would never wish that on you," he said.

He told her to remember the principle of carpe diem and to reverse the decision. It was as if the past came back, and he remembered when he wished that he could do all possible when she slipped away from him. "Do what is in your heart," he said.

Therefore, she called Yue yet again. Thinking he might be home. Then she called again. Again. In addition, she emailed him. And she emailed him again. And she called again every few minutes.

These are her emails to him:

"Ok, I admit I can't take this. We can stop these games now. We have proven to each other how much we care. We can make it. We do not need to separate to be able to make it. Talk to me. Call me.

I came to this conclusion after having talked with an ex of mine who still loves me. He told me that there is no time like the present. I will probably go crazy over you if I were not with you. I cannot promise to go slow, but I promise that I do not care about your age. I am strong. I'm a big girl."

Getting higher from the stash, their moods became elevated as she waited for Yue to be home. Because hope was fertile in her fields. The man who loved her told her that the euphoric feelings from getting high are similar to the euphoric feelings of being in love and that she was on a double high. He told her that was how he dealt with losing her.

She called again. When Yue answered the phone, he gruffly told her to read his email to her and that he liked what she said yesterday. Panicked, she tried to keep him on the phone and him, perhaps coming to believe that her love for him was genuine, answered all her questions. Afterwards, she read his email:

"It's over. Were I thirty years younger, there might be a chance. In a couple of years, I will begin the downhill aging process. In no way will I let you be saddled with an old man. You are young and have the whole world ahead of you. Grab on to it.

It's over."

That day was the day that it was over. Not the day before. That day it was over. Over. After more than 800 emails from him, it was the end. He threw her back into the sea with a great toss. It was the first time someone broke up with her. It was the first time since she had depression in high school that she would be one day without a boyfriend. However, even in the overness of the finality of the end, she felt pearls of hope. "If I were thirty years younger..." he said. "I will never forget you..." he said. "We will keep in touch..." he said. She noted, with a pang of sadness the addition of ten more years, the closing of his clamshell. On their first date he said, "If I were twenty years younger..." she had pearls of hope despite the fact that he said

"I do not love you" because, after all, a man should only say it when he absolutely means it. To lie would have been worse if it had been to give her hope and take it away at a later time. To lie so that she would let go and live her life, because she loved him so much and wanted to honor his wishes, was okay by her. He did not have to love her for her to love him.

Her heart was wrong, just like her father said, "You cannot trust your judgment."

She felt so much like a fool, wishing that he would forget her last moment of weakness and remember only, only their good times together.

"It hurts. It hurts. It hurts. Oh God, does it hurt! It will not stop hurting. It will never stop hurting!" she cried out in despair to the one who loved her. Her cries sounded like a toddler's or an infant's. Wishing to be twenty years older, she became twenty years younger.

She felt as Perez felt when she walked off and left him to pick up the pieces.

A sad song played from her iTunes. The man who loved her went to change the song, saying that it was the song that he listened to when they had broken up, years ago.

The man who loved her told her, "It only takes one person to love. You will never stop loving, but the pain will go away. You have to continue living. You have to learn to accept it."

"I wish he had Alzheimer's so that I could start anew with him," she said selfishly, "When he dies, I will have peace that he is all around me and can watch me. It will give me motivation to be a good, pious, God-fearing person. The first person I want to meet in heaven is him. When he dies, I will spend my yearly vacation on visiting his grave. He gardens, but he never told me his favorite flower. Else, perhaps, I forgot. It will be uncomfortable going to his funeral. People will ask,

'Who is that girl who cries like the sky has fallen on her head?' When I die, I wish to be buried next to him."

(May this be her living will and testament. Maybe she could be buried a little far from him, so she did not disrupt the family scheme, but close enough for the dirt above their graves to mingle as they decompose.)

She did not know if he were serious that they would be in contact again in the future. She wished that she had his seed then, if she were never to see him again. However, her period started, and it was a heavy flow.

He told her he would scan pictures of himself in his younger days months before he broke up with her, and she had yet to see one of those scanned pictures. He told her, repeatedly, that he would send her a telegram. He told her they would dance and cook and that he would give her a nude massage. He told her that he would visit her friend who was local to him, as a friend of a friend to update that person about her life so far. He never did. He was afraid of her commitment to him.

She hoped that within his complaint about age were many factors, as there typically are around any major decision. She hoped that within his worries about age were other fears and feelings, not just the topical one. She loved and hated that he had considered his daughters and had thought of what would be in their best interests. Would they have considered his decision to be in their best interests had they known? she wondered. Don't people who love each other want that person to be happy? She hoped that he remembered her counselor's advice and wanted her to gain confidence in herself through finding comfort in being alone. She hoped he remembered that she refused to make major decisions until at least a year had passed from when she left her ex because she truly needed a year of relaxation. She hoped that he remembered how she was taking care of a grown man as if he were a child before they had dated and that he did not want that for her. She found it ironic in the end, or at least this temporary end, that for someone who did not plan, he thought an awful lot about the future and the mysteries of the future when it came to her. She wished he understood the way she thought, and that they create the future in the present.

When she told her mother she said, "You are lucky to have two men who care for you. One man, your ex, gives you what you want. The other man, Yue, gives you what you need. If you truly love him, you will accept this gift he is giving you."

So, she printed out his email and laid it upright on the coffee table with a figurine pointing to it that said, "LOVE."

Since May she had lost two best friends: the man who wanted her to be his wife and the man who wanted her to be his girlfriend.

CHAPTER 28

Afterward

"Heartbreak"
I trust you,
so I tell you my secrets.
I tell you
how hard I have fallen
for your
sweet changing eyes.
I uncover my deepest fear,
the fear of living
without you,
but do so anyways.
I expound
about how life would not
be the same
if I considered you
a figment of my imagination,
a long-distance blip
in my long-term memory,
if I treated this relationship
the way you do.
I cannot read in-between
your folds of gray matter.
What you tell me,

what I hear,
is that you are closing,
closing off possibilities,
dreams, prayers, beliefs, desires.
All is logical
in your world.
Simple is logical.
Not to me—my logic
is simple,
even if it makes my life
complicated.
My logic is found
deep within her heart.

She bawled for two days, taking bathroom breaks during work, so she could cry. From then on, he soaked into her like the stain on a sponge. Never did a second go by that he was not in the background of her thoughts. Sometimes she woke up wondering if she had gotten any sleep.

The next day, she called the cable company to cancel her cable. She would not need the extra expense. She read her horoscope on Tarot. com. The advice given was too late in coming:

"Whether it's a job, deal or relationship, you're excited to get into it. Do not let that eagerness show. Play it cool. Otherwise, at the mention of the word 'commitment,' you just may hear the sound of feet hitting the ground."

And

"You can choose the path to take today -- even if it feels like you need to follow instructions or just go along with the crowd, you need to remember that you always have a voice, and you always can use it. So, if you are feeling under pressure from someone you are romantically interested in, follow your heart. Do not delve deep into any type of emotional entanglement right now unless you are completely ready. If you're not, then they'll just have to wait for you."

She did a tarot card reading for myself, and it said she did not see a way out of a problem, she wanted to get money together, she was an emotionally sensitive woman, and that she may tend to obsess about him in isolation. She played "Don't You Know" by Paul Hardcastle, and she thanked God for answering her prayers as a cruel joke. She was thankful for the pain, because the pain came from knowledge that would never leave her, the knowledge of what love is.

Her friends showed her support and took her out for distractions. A friend took her to the Renaissance Fair, which, of course, reminded her of Yue. That day she met a woman who was 40 who was used to dating men 20 years older. She confided to her a little, and she told her, from her own life experiences, that he was selfish and that he should mature.

Another person said he was just making up an excuse.

"Do you think that what he did was selfish or unselfish?" she asked her friend.
"I think it was a little bit of both," he said. The question prevalent in her mind was, did he do it thinking of me or of him? If she were to find later that his true colors were a bad shade of yellow, then she would console herself by knowing that even though she loved him, she did not have to like him. He made her decision for her exactly like a stereotypical birth parent or a parent that is about to spank a child, telling her, "I am doing this for your own good" or "This is going to hurt me more than it is going to hurt you." The meaning she heard was "Even though nothing is impossible, I just do not feel that I want to put that much energy, will, and determination into being with you. That is why you are better off not putting that much energy, will, and determination into being with me. I just do not feel the way you do." This analogic thought made her wonder if she should just give up trying to find her birth parents.

As she thought that, she thought of what her counselor had said to her about love and that to understand love one must understand more than romantic love. What she thought when her friend said what he had said was, yes, she thought that is how it is when birth parents let go—it is a little bit of both.

She also remembered what Yue told her, "The world and all that comprises the world, is differing shades of gray."

Another day her aunt took her to an old-fashioned diner. A song that just happened to be playing was "You're The One That I Want" from Grease, the musical. The following days, she comforted herself with various songs and ate lunch on the rooftop of the building where she worked. She would watch planes land at the nearby airport, wishing she were in one.

In the bus, the man sitting across from her was reading a book about learning Spanish. She commented, and he spoke to her a little about learning Spanish.

She asked the advice of a man who was 70 years old and always wore a blue ball cap on the bus. He told her that if he were Yue, he would have found a second wife. "He was a fool," the man said. Another time, on the bus, a boisterous 55-year old man who appeared at least ten years older than Yue or the older man she had talked to earlier boldly asked her, "Do you want to see me? I would like to see you. My wife died. I will not remarry. I have ten grandchildren. I have $10 million" because he was desirous of companionship.

Yue had too much pride to do something like that. Plus, he did not have that much money. She never sought his money.

She was sad that they did not last together until December.

CHAPTER 29

The End

"Extremities"
Yes, you caught me
at a bad time,
but somehow it was a
good time
to begin
something magical.
Against my better judgment,
we talked about
serious things,
things that had to be said
earlier rather than later,
but earlier could have been
just a little later.
We stayed at a high wattage,
like a sugar high,
but then *pop*
change occurred in you
before I could
compromise my position,
before I could say
either way
was fine.

You changed your mind
prematurely,
before I could.
Now I am left
with a changed mind,
but a constant heart,
constantly broken, yet
mended all at once,
healthy because you have
taught me important lessons.
I have learned
that I cannot warm
your cold feet.

"If you are out there and you are reading this," Zarah wrote, "know that I have accepted your gift of a 'better life,' but I will always love you. Love endures all. I will love you no matter if you share the same feelings for me. The above applies to you as equally as it applies to my birth parents.

The rest applies to you alone: Age just means that you are on earth a shorter time than me, but you (I hope) will be in heaven forever. Maybe you will finally believe me. As I have told you, you seem to have a thing for unhappy endings. I would love to change that about you. I would love to change your desire to be single. However, I have learned that I cannot change anyone. However, any man can change his own mind. As for guilt, it has no place in a relationship. Next time we will go slowly. I will always be your secret lover or your friend. I just want you nearby. True love waits. You have no idea how long."

* * *

As she stood waiting for her bus, a gray-haired man bent his back over to pick acorns off the ground. He stooped, bent, crouched to pick those acorns near and far—as many as he could find until the bus arrived. They all went into a grocery store plastic bag, which went into a duffel bag. Curious, she asked him what the acorns were for. He ignored her even though she was within earshot of him.

Contemplating the value of picking acorns, she realized the significance. Acorns represented those things she would need to plant, harvest, and collect if she were to be in a relationship or even if she were not to be in a relationship. They were those things that improve one's standing, that show one's determination and discipline. Money was a big one—so she could afford to shorten the physical distance, so they (whoever "they" is) could afford a future together, so she could afford a future and retirement apart if "they" were never meant to be. Then there are the invisible acorns—steps toward improving herself so that whether she were or were not to be with him, she would be ready to nurture and not destroy a potential relationship.

Yue and Perez, whether or not they loved her, had much more important acorns to gather. These acorns would require them to plan for the future despite their reluctance to do so, despite their desire to play by ear or by wind.

These acorns for Yue were more immediate than for her for he was already in the winter of life, or maybe the fall of life. His acorns were already past due. Whether or not he would wait for her, he needed to get into heaven even if by a different method than what he had already tried. Even after he died, she would pray that he would get into heaven had he been placed in purgatory instead. For how would she know if she had lost all contact? He had to go to heaven beyond all doubt. The acorns he needed to gather were steps leading to the Holy Christ, entries into Saint Peter's journal.

The acorns for Perez were more immediate than for her for his time was running out too. Time was running out to change bad habits, habits that could last throughout his lifetime, habits that could lead to an earlier death. Habits that could keep one in place, in the hole he built, in the quicksand, in the mountain prone to avalanches, and had to go soon. Perez needed maturity and to acknowledge what he was and the patterns he would repeat if he were aware of them.

* * *

She used her intuition a lot now and believed in it. She believed her intuition more than what she could see and hear. In the past those senses often deceived her and kept her in a place where she would rather not be.

There was a knock at her door. She opened it up. They looked at each other. She was as Black as a deadly scorpion in a desert, and he was virginally white, though not pale. The contrast of their skin reflected the contrast of themselves in the beginning. However, much time had passed, and they have seen transformations within themselves and around themselves, for all life emanates from within and not from without. And so, as selfish as he had been in the past, he decided to change his ways. That day he bestowed a gift to his dark beauty. "Here, this is for you," he said as he reached out his hand to her neck. In his clasped hand was a feather pendant necklace. The feather was pure white, like an absolute truth, alongside a ruby stone. It was truly a gift from the heart, for it was a gift that reflected who he had become.

He wrapped his right hand around her from the back of her neck to the front of her neck to in front of her vision. He steadied it with his free hand. However, as he struggled to put the necklace on her with the tiny clasp, he lost his grip on it, and it fell gently to the ground. As he dropped the feather, she noticed a fresh tattoo imbedded in his wrist. A scorpion's stinger peeked out from under his green long-sleeved shirt that had the word "Money" written across the chest in silver paint that looked like rhinestones. Somehow, the dropping of the feather necklace made her 100% certain that this would be the last memory she would ever have of him. She looked him in his eyes. He looked back, thinking that the look was loving and welcoming.

Then she closed the door.

It took a few seconds until his head wrapped around the action, then he started banging on the door and shouting, "What does he have that I don't have? Why? Why?"

* * *

A month after the breakup from Yue, the phone rang.

"Hello?"
"Hi." She recognized that voice.
"Hi," she said, melting.
"I miss you."
"I miss you too."
"Let's start over."
She looked over her shoulder to say goodbye to her ghosts.

For days afterwards, friends, family, and complete strangers would go up to her and tell her that she looked "radiant" and they would ask her for her secret. She would just smile and say, "love."

EPILOGUE

After reading this story, one can see the threads of emotional abuse from the first boyfriend. Zarah, the co-dependent, and Threat, the emotional abuser with Narcissistic Personality Disorder, led lives of hurt and anger. This story serves as a warning. Emotional abuse is more common than many believe even if the players involved vary.

The second arc dealt with commitment phobia. Zarah was the helper, and Yue was the doubter. Zarah and Yue led lives of passion and dreams. They also lived opposite lives of faith and distrust. This story serves as a warning to a different group of people. Commitment phobia is prevalent and only becoming more so in a country where, and in an age when, people wish to preserve their individuality, their freedom, and their privacy at the cost of their purpose in life, the true meaning of life.

Both warnings highlight the imperative need of hard work and faith if one wishes to rise above his or her sad station. The only way out of it, the only way to stop abusing, to stop going back to being abused again, or to stop hiding from what has real potential is to find love and respect for yourself. Sometimes the motivation to love oneself comes from another person, someone who helps that person believe again in love, life, and their own intuition. This person may be an imperfect person, for we all are, but anyone who gives respect deserves respect.

ACKNOWLEDGMENTS

Thank you to everyone I have spoken to in Codependents Anonymous. I will not name names in order to preserve your privacy. Thank you to everyone who has shared his or her experiences of being in an emotionally abusive relationship. Thanks go out to my counselor and other counselors I have met along the way. Thank you to everyone who has proven to me that I am not crazy.

Thank you to everyone I have spoken to who is or was in age-gap relationships of over twenty years' difference. Thank you to all those who love me and to those I love, even those who doubt my love. Thanks to God who showed me the way to understanding unconditional love. In addition, thanks to the man who told me it only takes one person to love. And thanks to the man I love and who loves me.

REFERENCE

D., Chuck. Fight the Power. Delta. September 8, 1998. p.44 and p.107.

ABOUT THE AUTHOR

Woo Ae Yi is a poet, screenwriter, and author. This is Yi's first book of prose. Yi's helped edit An Empty House (2008), a compilation of Korean-American poetry. Love, Not Love was Yi's first published book of poems. It came out in October 2008. Yi's second book of poems was Valley of the Mind's Shadow. It came out in April 2009. Lyrics and Verses and Fringe and Frivolity also came out that year. The Kindle version of Lyrics and Verses came out in March 2010. The Kindle version of Fringe and Frivolity came out in November 2010. Yi's first script, Escape from Crystal City, came out in July 2010. After Yi wrote this book, Yi published her seventh book, her fifth book of poetry, What Is This, Art Exhibitionistella? Her last book was Profiles of KAD Relations with the Black Community, a nonfiction book about Korean adoptee relations with the Black community in the time before and after George Floyd's death.

For more books please visit my website at www.yiwooae.com.